THE YOUNG PRETENDER

ALSO BY MICHAEL ARDITTI

The Celibate
Pagan and her Parents
Easter
Unity
Good Clean Fun
A Sea Change
The Enemy of the Good
Jubilate
The Breath of Night
Widows and Orphans
Of Men and Angels
The Anointed

Michael Arditti

THE YOUNG PRETENDER

or The Dramatic Return of Master Betty

First published in Great Britain in 2022 by

Arcadia Books
An imprint of Quercus Editions Limited
Carmelite House
50 Victoria Embankment
London EC4Y 0DZ

An Hachette UK company

A CIP catalogue record for this book is available
from the British Library.

ISBN (HB) 978 1 52942 255 9
ISBN (Ebook) 978 1 52942 256 6

10 9 8 7 6 5 4 3 2 1

Typeset by MacGuru Ltd in Garamond
Printed and bound in Great Britain by Clays Ltd, Elcograf S.p.A.

Papers used by Quercus Books are from well-managed forests and other
responsible sources.

For Louise Doughty and Bruce Hunter

1

On my last visit to this city in 1806, the Abbey bells pealed to celebrate my arrival. A band played beneath my window the following morning and Papa complained that they expected a perquisite. A lady of rank coaxed the hotel keeper into costuming her as a serving maid and setting her to wait at my table. I do not recall her name and doubt that she would thank me if I did. I was fourteen years of age.

I am six years older now, ten inches taller, and my voice has acquired that mannish crack of which the poet wrote. Should my name spark a recollection, my figure swiftly dispels it and I am able to enjoy the diversions of Bath unremarked. At eight each morning, I visit the Pump Room to take a draught of the water, which I am assured is salutary in despite of its taste. I tarry while the orchestra plays a selection of German airs, before strolling to the coffee house where I read the newspapers, conversing with my fellow patrons on matters ranging from the war in Spain and the quakes in America to the building of Queen Charlotte's Orangery. I parry any question about the object of my visit with a casual allusion to physicians and cures. We then part company as they make their way to breakfast with friends, followed by a morning concert or a scientific lecture, a game of billiards or piquet in the Assembly Rooms, a ride or drive in the countryside or a gentle promenade in the parades and arcades, while I go back to the hotel to address the business of the day.

I am making my return to the theatre. I have confided my purpose to no one for, while I am assured that the world at large will applaud it, I am aware of those who, professing to have my best interests at heart, would wish me to confine my endeavours to a domestic sphere. I shall allay their concerns. How could anyone who has heard the huzzahs ring in his ears seek to dissuade me? Then again, has anyone ever heard such huzzahs, save those notables with whom my name was once coupled? In Edinburgh, I was a second Chatterton; in Birmingham, a second Mozart; and everywhere, a second Garrick. The Young Roscius! The Wonder of the Age! A Player Sans Peer! The Prince of Wales received me at Carlton House and presented me with a coach and four. The greatest lords and statesmen of the day attended my performances and invited me to fetes and banquets. Painters painted me and poets eulogized me. Duchesses vied to drive with me in the Park. And all this before I had attained my fourteenth birthday. Then, before I had attained my fifteenth, they forsook me, forcing me to quit the stage when I had barely concluded the first act.

My renown lasted a mere eighteen months, but I am determined to recover it. Thus far I have sought to reacquaint myself with my surroundings. Every afternoon at four, I have made my way to Beaufort Square to be first in the line when the theatre doors are opened, even on Thursday when the cotillion ball in the Assembly Rooms attracts all but the most ardent playgoers. I hand over my three shillings at the pay box and take my check, to surrender it moments later at the pit door. After securing my place, I survey the house. I glance up at the ceiling, too distant for me to discern whether the winged figures, surrounded by discreetly undraped maidens, are angels or allegories. I turn to the one-shilling gallery, more mannerly here than in some parts but still inclined to employ the platform as a receptacle for their refuse. I lower my gaze to the boxes, the crimson-and-gold decoration eclipsed by the jewelled-and-silken splendour of the female occupants. While loath to censure their conduct, I wish that they would cease – or, at the very least, quiet – their chatter on the actors' entrance. I shuffle along the bench to accommodate the late arrivers, whose tardiness provokes protests from my neighbours. Nothing can destroy my own excitement, not even the pungency that permeates the house during the five hours in which the play is followed, first by the farce, and then by a medley of patriotic songs. It is the smell of floats and size and the actors' exertions and the crush of the crowd. It is the smell of my youth.

Soon, it will be the smell of my adulthood. For the first time in four years, I enter a theatre not as a spectator but as a player. I have been engaged for eight performances in Bath and two in Bristol by Mr Dimond, the circuit manager, whose correspondence is peppered with heartening recollections of my previous appearances, even if it dwells overmuch on the receipts. Our appointment is for eleven, but I arrive a half-hour in advance. I make myself known to the prompter, one Mr Charlton, but decline his offer to escort me. The stage is my element, as familiar to me as my bedroom at home in Pyms Farm. As ever, it is parsimoniously lit and I admire the scene-shifters' skill in manoeuvring the flat-scenes without incident. Narrowing my eyes, I make out a vista of the Royal Crescent, ready for the evening's performance of *The Rivals*, which is sure to draw a full house on its native soil. My heart aflutter, I step on to the platform, gingerly testing the grave trap into which I once leapt to gather the dead Ophelia in my arms. No one challenges me and the fancy takes me that I am one of the ghosts of bygone players who, according to green room lore, frequent the sites of their former glory. With melancholy looming, I remind myself that I am no incorporeal being, caught forever between roles, but a dispossessed heir – a Norval or a Selim – returning to his rightful domain.

A call boy heralds that return with his cry of 'Overture on, sir.' I turn around to find that he has vanished, while the voice in my ear deepens into that of Mr Dimond.

'Master Betty, forgive me. I have only just been apprised of your arrival. You are most welcome.'

'It is Mr Betty now,' I gently rebuke him, as I accept the proffered hand.

'Of course, of course. Forgive me. I would never have recognised you. You are taller . . . fuller.'

'I wish to be admired for the excellence of my representation, not the symmetry of my figure.'

'Of course, of course. But was it not ever thus? When I heard of your success in the north, I was incredulous. How could a boy of . . . what were you? Eleven?'

'In Belfast, yes. By the time we crossed the sea, I had turned twelve.'

'How could a boy of any age hold his own against full-grown players? I admit that when I first saw you, I was sensible of the discrepancy . . . the incongruity.'

'I recall very little and that only in flashes, as if I were standing on the stage while they moved the lamps. But I do recall that my entrance was greeted with laughter on several occasions. Mr Hough – my tutor – charged me to ignore it.'

'Very wise. In a matter of moments it was replaced by awe. The power of your playing silenced scoffers and sceptics alike.'

'I thank you.'

'I see you now as Norval,' he says, seizing back my hand as if to transport me to the scene of my greatest triumph. 'The refinement of your obeisance to Lady Randolph, which proved you to be no mean shepherd's boy. The rapture of your countenance when she disclosed the secret of your birth. Your righteous fury when you confronted the villain, Glenalvon. Your despair on realising that fate had restored your mother to you only to tear you apart:

"O had it pleas'd high heaven to let me live

A little while! – my eyes that gaze on thee

Grow dim apace! My mother—"'

He releases my hand to strike an attitude, a reminder that in his day he had been accounted a capital actor. 'Your youth, your freshness, your grace, your candour stirred every bosom.' The tears welling in his eyes enhance his words. I feel a pricking in my own, but it is my memory as much as my vision that is clouded.

'I am Mr Betty now,' I repeat.

He leads me to his office where, blowing the dust off a glass, he pours me some brandy. I take a nip but, catching sight of the mouse droppings on the floor, decline one of the Union biscuits that he munches blithely. We exchange pleasantries about the recent Christmas festivities, the new turnpike in Shropshire and the comfort of the York House hotel, although we are both as eager to attend to the matter in hand as the audience during a rambling prologue. After the requisite interval, he restates the terms of my engagement, setting out my nights. He declares that there are several members of the company who remain from my last visit and they, along with my many friends in Bath, will delight in my return. To my dismay, he has yet to announce the dates.

'On Wednesday I shall arrange for a judicious paragraph to be inserted in the *Chronicle*. The town will be caught unawares. I foresee that the box keeper's office will be besieged. Of course, we can expect nothing to match the frenzy that accompanied your previous appearances. No one – not Mr Kemble, not Mrs Siddons – has ever approached the appeal of Master Betty. The stampede at the doors was so great that, against all precedent, we were obliged to institute a lottery and sell tickets in advance. Even so, we escaped lightly compared to the theatres in the north. The newspapers blazoned accounts of the fury of those who failed to gain entrance . . . the deployment of the militia to quell the tumult . . . the woman who was killed in Liverpool.'

'Killed, just coming to the play?'

'But it was not just a play; it was Master Betty.' The thought disconcerts me and I gulp the rest of the drink. 'I admire your courage,' he adds, mistaking my fuddled look for equanimity. 'Other actors have to contend with the repute of their predecessors in old plays and the effects of their fellows in new; you have to contend with memories of yourself.'

'I am Mr Betty now.'

'No actor has ever been so esteemed, only to be so discarded.'

'I remember very little.'

'Yes, of course,' he says, with a smile that smacks of discretion.

I am speaking the truth. My memory has always been strong, which is how I was able to take on such taxing roles. They gave me my lengths and, within a few hours, I had them by heart, as if my mind were a mirror – no, not a mirror, for that would have inverted them and I never mistook a line. Yet, try as I might, I cannot recall why I fell from favour. I know that the houses were no longer full and, on some nights, the huzzahs did battle with hisses. I know that, in London, the managers no longer competed for my services. But everything else is a vacancy. Papa would scarcely speak to me, his silence betokening his disappointment and even his contempt.

It was left to Mama to explain that I was the victim of circumstance. The theatre is not a world set apart, and the news from abroad had overshadowed its proceedings. Buonaparte's armies had subjugated most of Europe. Britannia might still rule the waves, but the victory at Trafalgar had been scarred by Lord Nelson's death. I had witnessed for myself the outburst of dolour from the crowd when the royal barge bearing his coffin sailed up the Thames from Greenwich, followed by a flotilla of sixty boats, whose watermen held aloft their oars as though they were presenting arms. I was invited to watch the procession by Lord and Lady Abercorn, two of my foremost friends, but when I asked if we would be joined by Lady Hamilton, they looked shocked.

'I doubt very much that you will be hearing from that party again,' Lady Abercorn replied, as if offended by her mere existence. 'The siren has sung her last song.'

'His doctor attests that, with his dying breath, Nelson

left her and her bastard issue to the nation,' Lord Abercorn said.

'A gift more suited to an infidel seraglio than a Christian kingdom,' Lady Abercorn said, with a shudder.

Young as I was, I pitied the abandoned lady on whom, only months before, our hosts had fawned when we performed together at Abercorn House. Lady Hamilton exhibited her Attitudes, pantomiming the tragic heroines of Greece and Rome while enveloped in a vast white shawl, and I recited speeches from *Tancred and Sigismunda*. As we left, she clutched me to her bosom, which smelt of violets and wardrobes, kissing me wetly on the cheek. Soon we were both to be outcasts. Yet I will not allow the memory to distress me. Is it not a law of nature that anything that soars so high must suffer a commensurate fall, unless it is to vanish in the Empyrean?

I made my last appearance in London the following May and, for the next two years, I traversed the country, playing in towns and cities where fashion held less sway. Papa continued to bill me as the Young Roscius, a name that I grew to hate, not least when my cheeks filled out and my upper lip bristled, amid other palpable signs of manhood.

Now I am ready to return; I am everything that I was as a boy and more. I have known in myself the passions that hitherto I had to mimic: loneliness; loss; bereavement; betrayal; even love for Letty, my Cambridge sweetheart. Love, loss and betrayal, together with resentment, revenge, folly and pride, all feature in my first role, the Earl of Essex in Henry Jones' play. Mr Dimond's surprise that I have not chosen one of my more celebrated roles vindicates my choice. I may not be contending with the boy that I was, but I have no wish to court comparison. I first played Essex five years ago, not in London or Bath, but in Buxton, Carlisle, Dumfries and Cheltenham, and although there is little genius in the play, it contains passages of great power and excellent opportunities for points. The same is true of my other roles: Orestes in *The Distress'd Mother* and Tristram Fickle in *The Weathercock*.

Mr Dimond escorts me to the prompter's office, where Mr Charlton is instructing a copyist. After a few words of encouragement, he withdraws, swiftly followed by the copyist, leaving me to settle the stage business with the prompter. He begins by praising the excellence of the cast, discussing each one in turn with disquieting intimacy, as if I were a local dignitary whose support he was soliciting, rather than a fellow actor shortly to share their endeavours. He makes particular mention of Mr and Mrs Haughton, the doyens of the company, who are to play Burghley and the Queen in *The Earl of Essex*, and Phoenix and Andromache in *The Distress'd Mother*, with Mr Haughton also playing Old Fickle in the farce. They remember me of yore and 'are eager to see how Master Betty bears up.'

'They will have their wish,' I say, feigning a smile.

'You will have the pleasure of acting alongside Mr Clinch. He is to be your Southampton, Pylades, and Briefwit. He is a great favourite here, especially among the weaker sex. I am no talebearer, but he has found himself in pickles that it would task the pen of the most deviceful author to resolve. He too is impatient to meet the illustrious Master Betty.'

That impatience does not extend to a desire to rehearse. *Essex* has been played three times in Bath this season, and the company are willing only to attend two partial and one group rehearsal. I am not discouraged. My business is very simple and Mr Charlton jots it down on what looks like the back of an old handbill. I will make my first entrance with Southampton from the prompt-side door and fall to my knees before the Queen. She must beckon me to stand, enabling me to take my place at the centre of the platform. I then have no reason to move until the arrival of Lady Rutland, my wife, whereupon Mr Charlton interjects that, although not in the blush of youth, Mrs Whitefield is a most amenable actress who will not incommode my effects. In the great scene in the fourth act, when I strive to justify my conduct, it matters not whether she be to my left or my right, as long as she is a few feet in front of me, so that, in addressing her, I may address the house.

After agreeing on the procedure for the final act in which I am to appear in fetters, an innovation in Bath that I assure him will prove to be most felicitous, we part company, and I return to the hotel to rehearse in private.

Standing before the glass, I hear again Mr Hough's voice, as he prepared me for a speech.

'The Immortal Bard must have been jesting at the expense of his fellow actors, when he had King Duncan in the play, which we must not name – no, I said that we must not name it, William – remark that there is no art to find the mind's construction in the face. For every actor expresses his passions in his face and you are no exception. But, since they will be seen only by the most proximate spectators, you must perfect your gestures as well. Remember, your gestures must be as pleasing to the eye as your inflexions are to the ear.'

I do remember, as I assume the basic position, feet apart with the left forward and my weight resting on the right. I arrange my hands, ensuring that they are never at the same height, restraining my left, which as always seeks to usurp the precedence of the right. I recite Essex's first speech, genuflecting to the Queen, neck bent and right hand on my brow to signify my penitence. I raise both arms to bring out the force of the metaphor of 'th'all searching eye of heav'n,' before shrinking back from the Queen's frown, my arms thrust forward as if to ward off the terror. It is hard to judge the effect since, in lowering my gaze, I lose sight of the glass. For all my pains, I suspect that Mr Hough would still find fault.

'What have I told you about your hands?'

'To spare them?'

'To use them sparingly. You are not a drover rounding up his herd.'

'Ouch!'

I rub my ear, where he flicked it with his pages (never his hands) in a mixture of affection and exasperation. I rehearse for the remainder of the afternoon, grateful for the silent approbation of the glass, interrupted only by a furious knocking from my neighbours, whose own muffled moans and yelps I prefer to ignore.

After an excellent meal in the hotel dining room, among a party of naval officers home on furlough, I set off for the performance of *The Rivals*. I cannot recollect having seen it before and am charmed by its caprice, although I struggle to reconcile its carefree humour with the caustic wit of the Mr Sheridan, whom I subsequently encountered, worn down by the cares of management, at Drury Lane. The cast is creditable and I look forward to taking my place among them, although I am dismayed to discover that Mrs Whitefield has so far exceeded her youth that she plays the antiquated Mrs Malaprop. My only complaint is with the actor playing Sir Lucius, whose seesawing hands would surely have earned Mr Hough's rebuke and his impenetrable brogue have fuelled Mama's aversion to Hibernia.

Brushing aside my objections, I commend him as heartily as the rest when we gather in the green room the next morning. I approach each of the company in turn, extending my hand to the men and making my obeisance to the ladies, and am gratified by the friendly reception from all except Mr Cargill, whose coldness is understandable since I have assumed his role, relegating him to that of Raleigh.

Grateful for Mr Charlton's reminder of my association with the Haughtons, I greet them as old friends. They beam with the accustomed pleasure of country players at the notice of a visiting auxiliary. I smile as if I share their recollections of my previous engagement, when an apothecary ('no, it was a physician, my sweet'), who disparaged my playing, was driven out of the city, never to return, and a man who dared to laugh during my Romeo ('you mean Rolla, my dove') was at peril of being thrashed, until his neighbour declared that, far from mocking me, he had collapsed in delirium. My smile wavers when Mr Haughton, now with no spousal interruptions, recalls the two army officers who quarrelled so fiercely over the merits of my Selim that they resolved to fight a duel on Lansdown Hill, prevented only by the intervention of the justices. I am not so ingenuous as to suppose that Garrick himself lacked critics, but I am distressed that the officers should have aired their differences so violently. A duel over the merits of a player?

But it was not just a player, it was Master Betty.

Mr Charlton calls us to order and we begin to rehearse. The first hour is to be devoted to the business, and the second to the dialogue and the music. In line with several of my best loved characters, Essex does not appear until the second act, a delay that has always proved expedient for me, in both sparing my exertions and heightening anticipation. I enter with Mr Clinch and throw myself at Mrs Haughton's feet. She signals to me to rise and I wait while Mr Charlton bids her move to the right, allowing me to take my place at the centre of the stage. She argues that the Queen would never step aside for any subject and that Mr Cargill always walks down to the left, before adding that she 'will do anything to oblige dear Master Betty.' I express *Mister* Betty's thanks and take up the pre-eminent position, from which I rarely stir until the fifth act, when I am discovered within the scenes. Mr Cargill, who has affected an ignorance of Raleigh's movements that tires Mr Charlton's patience, snorts when he learns that I am to be fettered.

'The Earl is one of the premier noblemen of England, not a common varlet.'

'I assure you that the effect attracted widespread acclamation when I played the part before.'

'My dear sir, I trust that you will not expect the same indulgence to be given to the man as to the boy.'

'I crave no indulgence. Only the honest appraisal of my auditors and the support of my fellow players.'

My reply silences him, and the remainder of the morning's rehearsal passes without discord. After a short break for sherry and biscuits, we remove to the stage for our first and only group rehearsal. As I stand beside Mr Clinch at the proscenium door, I feel a shivering down my spine, a rush of blood to my temples and a tingling in my hands and feet. Yet it is neither excitement nor dread but rather a profound sense of belonging. I start to regret Essex's deferred entrance and fix my gaze on my fellow players, their expressions barely discernible in the shadows. All at once I make my way on to the stage, and Essex supplants Betty as I fling myself down before my queen with a fervour that startles my fellows, who adhere to the wretched practice of rehearsing under their voices and general powers. I am flustered only by Mr Cargill's mouthing of my lines, not just when he is in the side-wing but when, as Raleigh, he is with me on the stage. Assured by Mr Charlton that he will refrain on the night, I say nothing lest I provoke him.

Determined the next morning not to dwell on my impending labours and in accord with my usual custom, I repair to the coffee house, where I open the *Chronicle* to discover Mr Dimond's announcement of *The Return to the Stage of the Celebrated Young Roscius*. I cannot banish the fear that I will be forever yoked to the name, like the owner of the general stores in Ballynahinch, who remained Young Mr Gilchrist at fifty to distinguish him from his long deceased father.

The notice pricks the interest of my fellow patrons, who enter into a spirited discussion as to the wisdom of my return. Fearful of discovery, I remain aloof and catch only snatches of the exchange. I am perturbed when certain remarks incite laughter, in particular a tribute to 'golden hair gleaming in the lamplight and blue eyes ablaze with passion', which I presume to be mine, but I am reassured when one gentleman insists that he would not miss seeing my head on the block at any price. I wonder if some of them will recollect the reserved, soft-spoken man sipping his hot chocolate in the corner when, garbed in a black satin doublet with slashed sleeves and crimson velvet hose, I stride on to the stage.

I return to the hotel for a private rehearsal, but the room

feels cramped and oppressive. So, ignoring the February nip in the air, I take a brisk walk along the riverbank and recite my speeches to a herd of apathetic cows. At three o'clock, mind racing and body numb, I make my way to the theatre. Slowly my sensations return, although, as my legs shake, head shoots and heart pounds, leaving me drenched in sweat, I might wish that they had remained deadened. At a quarter before six, Mr Dimond knocks at my door to inform me that the house is almost full, amending the 'almost' to 'half' when, against my better judgement, I press him for particulars. Mr Hewitt, the stage manager, brings in the fetters, iron anklets secured by a long rod, borrowed from the local militia. I try them on and manage to attune my shivers to my shuffling steps. No sooner have I set them aside in readiness for the final act than Mr Haughton and Mr Clinch arrive, chatting gaily while I try to curb the chattering of my teeth.

Finally, the call boy comes to the door with successive cries of 'first . . . second . . . third music is rung, sir.' I trundle down to the side-wing and watch as Burghley and Raleigh instigate their conspiracy. When the act drop falls and the orchestra plays a short interlude, I feel as though the sequence of events has been reversed and, rather than returning from Ireland to throw myself on the mercy of the Queen, I am greeting my last dawn in the Tower. No prisoner doomed to the axe can have felt more trepidation than I do now. My throat goes dry, my mind blank, and my vision blurs. Mrs Haughton gives me my cue and I feel a sharp prod as Mr Clinch pushes me on to the stage.

The flurry of applause that greets my entrance revives me and I make my reverence to both the Queen and the house. The mark of approbation allows words to flow freely that I feared were forever locked inside my brain. I have the curious sensation that I am at the same time standing on the stage and watching myself from the pit, as Essex's determination to exonerate himself becomes my own:

'I came to clear my injur'd name from guilt,
Imputed guilt, and slanderous accusations.'

Although my legs remain unsteady, the power of the verse and the favour of the audience sustain me. Not even the sight of Mr Cargill, still mouthing my lines, can unsettle me. I receive two ovations in my first scene alone, and the clamorous demands of the pit and the gallery oblige me to repeat both my soliloquy at the end of the third act and my farewell to Southampton. When the curtain falls, I step forward to speak the epilogue, craving an indulgence that my listeners' response has long since rendered superfluous. I always dreaded having to speak in my own person, even when the words were written by Mr Hough. I am doubly uneasy now that they are mine. I make no claim to be a writer – hence my apprehension at embarking on this memoir – and wish that I had found more accomplished rhymes for 'Essex' than 'critics' and 'Betty' than 'fret ye', but the house appears content.

I return to the green room, where I receive the felicitations of my fellow players, although Mr Cargill continues to carp, asserting that the fetters induced a pathos that he aimed to achieve by acting alone. Mr Dimond admits a stream of visitors who, as ever, seek to enlist me in earnest discourse with no thought for the exertions which I have lately undergone. They each precede their remarks with recollections of my Hamlet, Osman, Selim and the inevitable Norval. A bewigged and bewhiskered lawyer who praises the manly vigour of my performance – and no epithet could gratify me more – asks why I did not choose a part more suited to my strengths, and I trust that it is fatigue that makes me discern a contradiction. A clergyman, with clumps of white hair like a cauliflower, supposing that his cloth grants him licence, pokes me in the stomach and asks if I plan to play Falstaff. A lady with a squint declares that seeing me anew is like returning to a childhood home sequestrated by creditors and then, as if to account for the metaphor, presents me with her latest volume of verse. I thank her and, pleading exhaustion, retreat to my dressing room, where I am determined that, henceforth, no stranger shall intrude.

In vain I try to marshal my impressions, sitting in a stupor until roused by Mr Clinch's rhythmical knock. Declining the invitation to join him and 'a pretty pair of petticoats' at the King's Arms (any regrets dispelled by his leer), I divest myself of my sodden costume and return to the hotel, where, for the first time in weeks, I pass the night like Richmond rather than Richard before the battle.

I wake to find that word of my performance has spread throughout the city. As I follow my morning regimen, I am greeted with doffed hats and gracious nods in the parades, handshakes and curtsies in the Pump Room, and pats on the back and convivial banter in the coffee house, where I am accounted respectively, a sly dog, a dark horse and an old fox. Many of those who salute me admit that they failed to attend the play, a delinquency that will now be remedied. Indeed, on entering the theatre, I learn from Mr Dimond that every box for my subsequent nights has been taken, and he expects large crowds to gather at the pit doors. The winter season in Bath is said to be the herald of the London spring, and he is confident that I will enjoy a similarly cordial reception in the capital.

Elated, I retire to my dressing room and practise my lines, eager to replicate the effects that found favour the previous night. A rap on the door announces Mr Clinch, who begs leave to converse with me privily. Assured that he has cast off his green room swagger, I invite him to take a seat. I await his jibes at the foibles of our fellow players but, instead, he plies me with questions about the Covent Garden and Drury Lane of my youth. Although I am resolved to put the past behind me, the candour of his sentiments disposes me to respond.

He reveals that he too trod the boards as a boy, on the Worcester circuit where his father was manager, but his roles (Prince Arthur and Richard, Duke of York) were commensurate with his age. A mere four years my senior, he followed my progress with interest and, he freely admits, envy. He read every memoir, critique and newspaper report that he could find, which is more than I did, since Mama kept them from me lest they turn my head. Yet, as he cites the accounts of my meteorical rise, untutored genius and native wit, I wonder if it were rather that she wished to spare me the untruths.

I laugh out loud as he relates the story – so affecting that he has it by heart – of my rescuing an actor who fell through a trap in Sheffield, and visiting him every day for a month while he recovered. With my memory as ragged as a supernumerary's hose, I accept that an actor may have fallen and even that I may have gone to his aid, but the month of visits is quite impossible since, the metropolis apart, I never remained in any city for more than two weeks. I fail to make out his expression in the shadows, but his drooping shoulders convey his disappointment. It is at that very moment that I determine to record my own impressions of my return to the stage, along with such memories of my childhood as I am able to retrieve. They are too important to be left to untrustworthy chroniclers. Both the boy I was then and the man I am now merit more.

2

Mama insists that she is not angry with me but disappointed. In the year since Papa's death, I have tried my utmost to live the life that she ordained for me. I practised archery and joined the Shropshire Hunt. I paid calls on the local families, taking tea with a string of eligible young ladies, whose fascination with my performances bolstered my desire to resume them. Mindful of her disapproval, I informed Mama that I had been invited to Bath to celebrate the majority of one of my Cambridge confrères. Aware for her part that I found rustic society dull, she encouraged me to make the trip. In the event, I suspect that she would rather I had purchased a commission in the Fifty-third and set sail for the Peninsular than set foot again upon the stage.

After a week of tacit reproaches, I ask her to accompany me on a stroll by the river (leaving a furious Marianne behind). I explain that I am in earnest about reviving my career and have written to several theatres, offering my services and enclosing Mr Dimond's copies of the Bath receipts. I have yet to hear from Covent Garden or Drury Lane but have been engaged to play for three nights in both Gloucester and Worcester. She shudders and drops my arm, hurrying along the bank as if seeking to compose herself. A moment later I follow her.

'Why are you so opposed to my most heartfelt desire?'

'I have no wish to see you hurt again.'

'Why "again"? When was I hurt before?'

'How much do you remember?'

'I remember being fatigued, of course . . . exhausted. I remember falling ill and the Duke taking me to recover at Bushy Park. But I was never hurt.'

'Not even when everything came to such a precipitate end?'

'But it was you who explained it. The death of Mr Pitt, following so soon after that of Lord Nelson, was deeply felt, even by the most diehard Whig. Added to that was the War, no longer just with France but with Prussia. People had greater concerns than the theatre.'

'I explained all that?'

'Who else?'

'I am glad.'

'You never wanted me to act, did you, Mama?'

'It was so long ago. You are a different person now.'

'No, merely an older one. I do remember some things . . . at least I am starting to. I can see you in a hotel room – I have no idea which or where – arguing with Papa as you beg him to remove me from the stage.'

I gasp, as I first hear a slap and then see a hand on her face. I must have confused it with something else – something I saw in a play: Mr Kemble as Othello striking Desdemona. But the hand is white and bears Papa's ring, stamped with the family crest of which he was so proud and which I now wear in his stead. I hear myself, insensible to her distress, fearful that she might succeed in her design. 'I hate you, Mama,' I yell, moving to Papa to manifest my allegiance.

'I love you, Mama,' I say, kissing her cheek.

'What did I do to deserve that?' she asks. 'There is no

need to appease me. You will be of age in September. You are your own man.'

'Even so, I would like your blessing.'

'You know you have that whatever you decide.'

We stand, gazing at the trout in the limpid water and, after a brief silence, commence a desultory conversation about poachers. Then, drawing her shawl tightly around her shoulders, she complains of the cold and we return indoors: she to the parlour to mollify Marianne; I to the study, which I still struggle to think of as mine. It is not just that Papa's books fill the shelves, and his papers, which I have yet to examine, fill the desk and cupboard, but his presence is as palpable as the cigar fumes that cling to the carpets and curtains. I see him smile wryly, as I move to the shelf where he has ranged the memoirs and pamphlets written during my boyhood. I count fifteen, one of which is 150 pages long (although in blessedly large print) and three of which are in verse. How many young men of twenty are graced with so many remembrancers? But then how many young men of twenty have so much to remember?

I was just sixteen years old when I fulfilled my last engagement in Gosport or Deal or Dover or whichever country theatre Papa had found, where the smile of fame outweighed the frown of fashion. The Young Roscius took his final bow at an age when the common run of players had yet to take their first. I felt as bereft of Norval and Selim and Tancred and Hamlet, as if they were brothers-in-arms dispatched by Buonaparte's soldiers. Papa did nothing to reassure me. Whereas other fathers watched proudly as their sons became men, mine lamented every sign of my maturity. Once in Bath, during a concert in my honour arranged by Signor Rauzzini, the director of music with the piercingly high-pitched voice, Mr Hough muttered that I was fortunate not to be a singer or Papa would have condemned me to the like fate. I apprehend his meaning better now, although it says more about his singular sense of humour than Papa's conduct towards me. Nevertheless, he showed a marked indifference to my future, raising none of the expected objections to Mama's proposal that I follow her brothers and matriculate at Christ's College, Cambridge. It was her foremost wish that I should take Orders. Where better than a country parsonage to bury the memory of Covent Garden and Drury Lane?

She sought to convince me by reminding me how eagerly I had attended Sunday worship in Ballynahinch, secure in our front pew, as disappointed when the sand in the pulpit hourglass ran out as Papa was incensed when the rector turned the glass over. With the pulpit the only platform left open to me, I saw no purpose in explaining that my interest lay less in the rector's substance than his style. Long before I ventured into a theatre, I was gripped by his emphases and flourishes, his swooping inflexions and sudden pauses, so painful to the village boys at the back of the church, whose every fidget would incur the verger's rod.

I remained at Christ's for two years and a half. I made few friends among my fellow gownsmen, who were afraid of being branded tuft-hunters. But there was one, Harness, who was oblivious to such censure. A boyhood accident had left him lame, a debility he offset with a nimbleness of wit superior to that of all our comrades. His twin passions were the Bible and Shakespeare, both of which he read for several hours a day. I was ignorant of all but the most familiar beauties of the former but thought that I could match him with my mastery of the latter. He swiftly disabused me, decrying the arrogance of 'a strutting mummer'. He pointed out that much of what I believed to be by Shakespeare had been imposed upon him by editors. My first scene as Crookback, when I set off to murder King Henry in the Tower, had been cobbled together by Cibber; my last scene as Romeo, when Juliet wakes before the poison I have swallowed takes effect, was an invention of Garrick's. I hesitated to invite further scorn by remarking that the scenes are nonetheless powerful, with both my hunger for Henry's head and my death in Juliet's arms never failing to elicit applause.

Harness disapproved of my going down without taking my degree, even when I explained that I wished to be with Papa during his mortal illness. How much more severe would he have been had he known that I had no use for a black silk hood, having privately resolved to reclaim the more colourful costumes of my youth! Before we parted, I promised to attend the ordination of the future Archbishop of Canterbury, for so I teased him. Who knows if he will set aside his prejudice and attend my coronation as Richard or Henry or Macbeth?

Like the underplot of a play, there was a secondary reason for my leaving Christ's: one that I could not admit to Harness, who had sworn himself to celibacy. I had developed a tendresse for Letty Hopkins, the daughter of our lodging-house keeper. She was – nay, is – beautiful and modest and grave and of a signally sweet nature. The mere thought of her, more than a year after our parting, is apt to draw forth the tears that I once spilt so carelessly for Juliet. I grant that she was just fifteen, but no one has more cause than I to ignore such distinctions.

Our attachment was favoured by her mother who,

trusting to my honour and Letty's prudence, offered us the freedom of her parlour. We took pains never to display any sign of affection in company, nonetheless word of our amity reached the ears of the Dean, who accused the blameless Letty of schemes more suited to the wanton creatures who ply their trade about Parker's Piece, and insisted that any further association with her would destroy my character. He allotted me a room within the college, its cell-like dimensions underlining my disgrace. I wrote once – sometimes twice – a day to Letty, but she, whose unschooled hand had enchanted me, never replied. Then Mama apprised me of Papa's illness and, although she cited it as a reason for me to apply myself to my studies and make him proud, I took it as an excuse to return home.

It is not yet nine months since he died, so I realise that my sentiments may be coloured by my loss, but I doubt that, even at the height of my fame, Papa was proud of me. He may have been proud that others were proud of me, but that is not the same. Poets had lauded me as Albion's favourite son but, if I were his, it was only because I lacked a brother. Even when dukes and duchesses crowded my dressing room, he railed that he had exchanged the honourable life of a gentleman for that of a fair-keeper. Yet when the fair was over and he could retire to Pyms Farm to devote himself to those same country pursuits that Mama maintains should now satisfy me, he hankered after the metropolis. He drank far more than was wise and, according to my sister Marianne, he was not always kind to Mama (although when I put the charge to her, Mama insisted that it was just a child's misapprehension and refused to discuss it). His liver was tumoured and, by the time of my return from Christ's, he was confined to his bed. The man whose black looks could make me quake, even when I was attired as Richard III or Osmond, was as yellow and shrivelled as an autumn leaf. He vomited more than he ate and lay in deathly silence for hours on end, before howling like a tethered dog in a thunderstorm. Should I be present during one of his rare moments of lucidity, he would either bewail my ingratitude to a father who had devoted his life to my welfare or beg my forgiveness for a chain of events that he had failed to foresee.

Attending Papa in his agony, I understood why audiences took solace from stage deaths, by sword or musket or poison, which, however sanguinary, were swift. He lingered on for six months after my return, breathing his last in June. Mama's dry-eyed relatives filled the pews at his funeral. When the lawyer arrived the following week to read the will, I was astonished to hear no mention of Pyms Farm, whereupon Mama explained that it already belonged to me.

'Everything Papa bought – indeed, everything he spent – was yours. Every jewel I possess that was not my mother's came from you. You fed us and clothed us and housed us . . .' Her words were drowned in sobs.

'That makes me so happy,' I said, stroking her hand. 'You and Marianne shall want for nothing as long as I live. And beyond,' I added, conscious of the document on the table.

'Promise me that you will think none the worse of Papa. He was a good man, even if he did not always show it.'

'Of course,' I replied instinctually, struggling to suppress a line that had crept into my head.

Why should I ever know my father, if he is a villain? My heart is satisfied with a mother.

*

— 26 —

I choose one of the memoirs at a venture and open it, eager to recover myself in its pages. After several allusions to *genius, virtuosity* and *brilliance*, augmented by *majestic, illustrious* and *beyond compare*, I blush as though I were once again being bussed by a covey of duchesses. I put down the book and pick up a second and then a third, only to find more of the same. I am not unmindful of the accolades but, after the confusion caused me by Mr Clinch's anecdotes, I am hungry for facts.

My origins are not in dispute. I was born on 13 September 1791, the son of William Henry West Betty, for whom I was named in every particular, and Mary Stanton. I sense the relief with which all the writers relate that both my parents were of gentle birth and possessed of handsome fortunes, as if to remove any stain of exigency from my endeavours. I was christened at St Chad's, Shrewsbury, and several of the memoirs reproduce the entry from the church register, which strikes me as redundant until I recall that Papa was obliged to furnish it to counter calumnies on both my age and gender. Most record that I spent my infancy at my mother's estate of Hopton Wafers in this very county, while adding nothing to my understanding of its loss. I know only that it was through some ill-advised venture of Papa's, which earned him the lifelong antipathy of my Stanton relatives. Mama, as always, was steadfast in his defence. 'Your poor father,' she said; 'he was not cut out for the world of affairs,' a view which I doubt would be echoed by many of the theatre managers of his acquaintance.

When I was four, Papa removed the family to his native county of Down in Ulster, where, according to the diverse accounts, he either purchased a farm and a linen factory or occupied his paternal property. None of the chroniclers paints a detailed picture of the district in which I was to spend the next nine years. It is as if, like Mr Hough, they wish to gloss over my association with Hibernia.

My own memories of Ballynahinch and its surrounds are few but vivid. I see the rows of grey stone cottages, smell the peat smoke in the bracing air, and hear the dulcet voices of the women, singing to each other as they spin the flax for Papa's factory. In a trice, that bucolic image shatters, and the smoke is that of the cottages engulfed in flames and the voices those of the women keening over their husbands, sons and brothers killed in the Rebellion. There are bodies scattered about the streets and pigs chomping on them, which Papa, resplendent in the blue-and-gold uniform of the Castlewellan yeomanry (am I being fanciful or is that blood caked on the sleeve?), takes me to inspect, dismissing Mama's concern that it is too harrowing a vision for a seven-year-old boy. Worst of all, so deeply imprinted on my memory that he returns even now in the hush of night, is the rebel strung up from the sail of a windmill, his decaying corpse swinging back and forth in the breeze.

What was it that first drew me to the stage? Some of the writers claim it was watching Mama and her sisters perform in private theatricals; others that it was hearing Papa's recitation of Wolsey's Farewell to all his Greatness, his favourite speech of Shakespeare's. It shames me that I can remember neither, although it may be they are as much a part of me as learning to walk and talk. I put the matter to Mama at supper.

'In the memoirs of my early life—'

'This is still your early life, William; you are twenty years old.'

'I know.' I check my impatience. 'They say that I watched you enact scenes with your sisters.'

'What nonsense! That is the reason I never read them. Your aunts would be horrified by any suggestion that they took part in plays. Besides, they never visited us in Ireland. They did not care for your . . . the climate.'

'But you did teach me to recite.'

'I taught you everything.'

'I know.' I smile at eight-year-old Marianne, who is presently receiving similar instruction, insulated from the village children with their hornbooks, their *crisscross-rows* and their *ABCs*.

'I drilled you in passages from the finest authors. Do you recall:

"From brightening fields of ether fair-disclosed,

Child of the sun, refulgent Summer comes."'

'*The Seasons,*' I say, feeling a glow as if summer had arrived in earnest and not just in verse.

'I was determined to expunge any hint of the ungentlemanly burr that might creep in from your daily discourse with the servants. I had no thought of fostering your histrionic skills.'

'And do you regret it?'

'That is not what I said.'

'What about Papa?'

'What about him?'

'Is it true that he used to recite Cardinal Wolsey's speech from *Henry VIII*?'

'Perhaps once or twice. You must bear in mind that, when those memoirs were written, he was being attacked for neglecting your education.'

'But he did not write them!'

'Of course not! Though he conferred with the men who did.'

'So, if their accounts are partial and my memories are fitful, what can I trust?'

'Your mama. You can always trust me, which is why I beg you to renounce this fancy of returning to the stage.'

'I have accepted the engagements. I am expected in Gloucester on the eighth of May.'

'I would like to see William in a play,' Marianne interjects. 'I was too young before.'

'You still are,' Mama replies, more tartly than is her wont.

'Never mind.' I console my downcast sister. 'As soon as you are ready for bed, I shall come up and read to you one of Mr Lamb's *Tales from Shakespeare*.'

'*The Winter's Tale*,' she says, choosing her favourite, and I speculate again on what took place during my absence in Cambridge to make her prefer the story of a jealous tyrant who mistreats his wife and seeks the death of his daughter, only to be reconciled to both by a seeming miracle, to the romance of *Romeo* and the magic of the *Dream*. Or is it just the excitement of the ravening bear?

'Not too late now,' Mama says, reasserting her authority, 'if you want to come to Wem with me in the morning.'

As master of the house, I retire to the study, pour myself a glass of brandy and light a cigar, both of which accord more with my new-found status than my taste. Reflecting on my afternoon's reading, I find that the one thing on which both the memoirists and my memory agree is that, no matter who spurred my interest in the stage, it was Mrs Siddons who sealed it. Papa, having affairs in Belfast and learning that she was playing in Mr Sheridan's *Pizarro*, took me to see it, although, in truth, I think that he was less curious to witness the inimitable actress than to hear Rolla's famed speech to the Peruvian army. With Buonaparte's forces on the verge of invasion, it had been hailed as a clarion call to arms: one which, as I could subsequently attest, never failed to draw forth a torrent of applause.

Peering across the narrow, filth-strewn street that led from Arthur Square to the theatre, I could have no inkling that, in less than three years, I would be uttering the speech myself and upon the very stage where the play had first been given. I sought Papa's hand – only for him to wrench it away – as we entered the building, strode through an ill-lit, sloping tunnel, climbed a small flight of steps, and found ourselves facing the platform. I stood spellbound, gazing up at the gilded boxes and ornamented ceiling, wondering why anyone should have wished to paint the heavens indoors. Papa, vexed as ever to see me abstracted, gripped my arm and led me to the front row of the pit. We took our places in the centre of the bench, securing them stoutly against the men who pressed us, pushed us and clambered over us. We waited for the first strains of the orchestra, with more patience than the denizens of the gallery, who assailed the stage with oranges, cheese rind and coins, thus obliging a servant, still dodging the missiles, to sweep it clean before the play began.

At last the curtain rose, revealing a lady who, from the prolonged ovation, I took to be Mrs Siddons. Thenceforth, whenever she was on the stage, she consumed my attention. I was moved by Rolla's unrequited love for Cora and Cora's desperate search for her missing son; I was roused by Rolla's rallying cry to his troops and thrilled by his courage in sneaking, disguised, into the Spanish camp and exchanging costumes with the imprisoned Alonzo. But they were as nothing to my enthralment to Elvira's every word and gesture. I sat transfixed as she implored Pizarro for mercy on Alonzo, vowed to abandon him forever, and plotted to wreak revenge. I watched as she urged the soldiers to torture her in retribution for her illicit love, oblivious of the tears streaming down my cheeks, until Papa, with a look of disgust, handed me his pocket square.

I returned home, ablaze with the excitement of the play. From then on, all the adventures that I had enjoyed with Gil Blas, Peregrine Pickle, Roderick Random and the rest paled by comparison. I no longer wished merely to read about a character's exploits; I wished to enact them. So I turned to Papa's new edition of the works of Shakespeare, the dark blue leather binding, gilt-edged pages and, above all, lavish illustrations heightening the allurement.

I doubt that I understood more than one word in ten and even Mama grew impatient with my requests for elucidation, but I was undeterred. As with the rector's homilies, it was the richness and rhythm of the verse, rather than its meaning, that captivated me. Like acidulated drops, both sweet and sour, it had a flavour all its own. To the irritation of the housemaid, I turned my bedsheets and bed-hangings into a front curtain; to the irritation of the gardener, I took plants and shrubs from the gardens to decorate the scenes; to the irritation of the cook, I took pots and pans from the kitchen to serve as headgear. No doubt to the irritation of Papa, I recited speeches to any passing adult. I longed for nothing more than to translate my efforts to the stage, but the height of my ambition was a juvenile role, like that of the boy who escorted his blind grandsire to the Peruvian camp in *Pizarro*. I never dreamt of playing the hero.

'I shall surely die if I may not be a player!' is the claim that, without exception, the chroniclers ascribe to me in my campaign to convince my parents of my resolve (I can vouch for the authenticity of the sentiment if not of the syntax). At first, they employed every argument at their command to dissuade me from a course so far removed from their own hopes for my advancement in life. Then, to my surprise, I read that *the father who fervently loves him*, perceiving that opposition was vain, surmounted his prejudices against a profession that was *in itself of the highest respectability but frequently degraded by the irregular and imprudent conduct of its members.*

I am prevented from pondering the paradox – indeed, the contradiction – by a bellow from Marianne to come upstairs and read her the promised story. Hastening to obey, I delineate the various characters more vividly than usual and receive as many requests to repeat my growl, when the bear tears into Antigonus, as I did for my most popular points on the stage. Finally, Mama enters and, deaf to Marianne's pleas, snuffs out the candle. Still intent on conveying her displeasure, she accuses me of overexciting the child. I wonder if, privily, she fears that Marianne may come to emulate my passion, a self-styled Young Roscia. The prospect makes me shudder, but it is not just for Marianne. Somewhere, although I have no recollection where, I have heard the appellation before.

In the parlour, Mama takes up her work and begins to sew. At the risk of distressing her further, I seek her help to shed light on the many obscure passages of my story.

'The memoirs—'

'Oh no, William, it is late.'

'It is barely eight o'clock! I have waited so long to make sense of everything; I never realised how long until Bath.'

'Very well. Although I doubt I shall be of use. My memory is not what it was.'

'It will still be clearer than mine. I was eleven when I made my debut – ten when I started to practise. But how did it come about? How did I go from bed-hangings and flowerpots in the drawing room to the Belfast stage? Some of the memoirs say that Papa took me to recite for Mr Atkins and I made such an impression on him that he introduced me to Mr Hough; others that Mr Hough came to tutor me before taking me to meet Mr Atkins.'

'That I can verify.'

'Which?'

'That Mr Hough tutored you first.'

'Did you seek out his services?'

'Why should it concern us now?'

'Please, Mama!'

'I think that Papa met him at the races. There was a course at Downpatrick, which he frequented, especially after the factory closed. It was his habit to bring people to Springhill – people who in the old days . . . no matter! Mr Hough was there with several players from Belfast. Papa invited them to dine with us on their way back to the city. After showing them his cups – ' she glances at the cabinet in which the fencing trophies of Papa's youth are proudly displayed – 'he must have remarked that he had a son with a zeal for the drama, at which the players, knowing what was required of them, called on you to recite. I sought to prevent it—'

'Mama!'

'I wished to protect you, William. Moreover, it struck me as an unwarranted imposition on our guests. But not for the last time Papa overruled me.' I shudder, as I once again hear the slap. 'You were summoned to the drawing room and, without a shred of reticence, recited a harrowing speech about torture.'

'Elvira,' I mutter under my breath.

'After which the players felicitated you, as they might any child in whose house they were to partake of a roast goose. All except for Mr Hough—'

'He was not a player.'

'No, he was the prompter. Not that I knew that then. He stood stock-still and extolled your excellence.'

What a handsome boy! I hear again his voice: gruff, with a harrumph at the end of every speech. *What a handsome boy!* No, I am misrepresenting him. What an accomplished boy . . . What a superior boy! *What a handsome boy!*

'Are you quite well, William? You look pale.'

'It is just the lamp. Is that when Mr Hough came to stay?'

'No, he left with the others and returned a day or so later. With no word to me, Papa had engaged him to tutor you. He – Mr Hough, that is – was so convinced of your talent that he offered to do so for no more than his daily fare. Which, as you may imagine, well suited Papa. I was apprehensive. After the recent insurrection in Dublin, theatres across the land were closed. Mr Hough was one of many who had lost employment. I feared that his admiration for you was hollow. Yet it seemed heartless to deny you the opportunity. I had kept you to myself for too long, refusing to allow Papa to send you to board at the Academy in Belfast, let alone to school in England. Besides, I felt sure that your fascination for the stage was a caprice and, as soon as you were set to work, you would lose interest. So I quashed my misgivings and welcomed Mr Hough.'

'Did you not care for him?'

'He always behaved very properly towards me. And it would have been wrong to condemn the man for the distress into which he had fallen: the want of soap and tooth powder and a clean shirt and kerchief, which offended the servants more than it did me. I even grew reconciled to his gimlet eyes and grim aspect. Papa assured me that he was a gentleman. As a youth, he had been admitted to one of the Inns of Court. But he neglected his studies to attend the theatre.'

'Which is when he saw Garrick. He never forgot it.'

'As well we know.'

'He used to tell me how much had been lost since Garrick's day. He was no admirer of Mr Kemble. "He should have been a mathematician. Those are the principles by which he acts. Right angles, perfect proportion, correct degree. He scans the verse rather than speaks it. I doubt that he knows what feeling is. Harrumph." Are you all right, Mama? You are trembling.'

'It is nothing. You sounded so like him.'

I realise that, without intending it, I have echoed not just the cadences of Mr Hough's speech but the tones of his voice, tones drummed into my consciousness until they rang in my ears each time I stepped out on the stage. 'I recall his voice better than anything else. Rough yet resonant. He should have been a player himself.'

'He was. We discovered some time later that he had tried and failed. He had abandoned the Law, whereupon his father – less indulgent than Papa – cut him off. We thought that he was helping you to fulfil your dream when, in truth, you were helping him to fulfil his.'

'Might they not have been the same?'

'He was fifty years old.'

'One of the memoirs claims that I called him my guardian angel.'

'In which case you were not the only one he tutored.'

Conscious of her discomfort, I change tack. 'I do remember meeting Mr Atkins. He was bald with a briary beard, and I spent much of the time picturing his head turned upside down so that he had a full head of hair and a shaven chin. Have I said something to upset you?'

'No, of course not,' she replies, dabbing her eyes. 'It is just that you were a boy. An eleven-year-old boy. You should have been at home playing boyish games.'

'I was so happy, Mama.' She smiles. 'As happy as a king. Mr Atkins led me on to the stage and then sat at the back of the pit. I recited the speeches that Mr Hough had chosen. But however much he admired my rendition of . . . who was it: Rolla? Osman? Norval? I still find it hard to credit that he engaged me.'

'Mr Hough could be very persuasive.'

'I cannot be sure – of anything – but I have it in mind that, within a matter of weeks, I had joined the company, acting alongside men twice my size and three times my age. For all Mr Hough's persuasiveness, Mr Atkins must have seen something singular in me to take such a risk.'

'Of course he did. You had great gifts, William. Extraordinary gifts. But that is not to deny that he was looking for some novelty with which to attract the town. The theatres had only just reopened. Emmett, the villain who had led the Rebellion, was still at large. You were a boy with no taint of an Irish accent, an emblem of resistance to enemies both at home and abroad. Mr Hough convinced Mr Atkins that you would make him a princely profit, just as he had done Papa.'

'So I was a mere gewgaw. A curiosity?'

'No, of course not. That is not what I meant. You have exhausted me.' She puts her needle and stitchery in her workbox, stands and approaches me. I bow my head to receive her kiss. 'Forget the past. You are in the flower of life. You have a fine estate and an ample fortune. You will have a wife and children. What more can you wish?'

'Nothing, Mama,' I say dully.

She goes out but, far from following her upstairs, I sit by the fire and ruminate. No doubt my youthful performances were marred by myriad faults, yet I made up in ardour for what I lacked in art. It was widely held that I was a natural actor, the first since Garrick, but that was only half-true. The expression, which I trust was natural, was indeed my own; the conception was Mr Hough's. With some passions I required little help; I think of Norval's and Osman's resolve to defend their mothers and even Hamlet's reconciliation with Gertrude, once he admits her guilt-less of his father's death. Nor did I need any prompting to convey Frederick's indignation at Baron Wildenhaim, when my own father was working me so hard. But for the rest I relied on Mr Hough. He taught me the rules with his customary precision.

'The principal passions in any tragedy are love, sorrow, anger, resentment, jealousy and revenge. Every babe out of napkins is familiar with the first three but, as yet, you have seen too little of the world to know the others. So you must pattern yourself on me, who has known them in his very marrow.'

His assurance was not misplaced. Whether or not my debut was greeted by quite the *reiterated and tumultuous applause* that one memoir records, and the next day *the name Little Betty formed the sole topic of conversation in all parts of the town* that is the assertion of another, it caused a sufficient stir for Mr Atkins to engage me to follow Osman with Norval, Rolla and Romeo in swift succession. Word of my success reached Dublin, and the manager of the Crow Street theatre contracted me for nine nights. From there, I was engaged to play in Waterford, Limerick and Cork. In the last of these, I was party to an incident that had a profound impact on my boyhood imagination.

A tailor in the town had been hanged for theft. After he was cut down, an actor in the local company succeeded in reviving him by rubbing his neck and chest with rum. As far as the authorities were concerned, the sentence had been carried out, and the tailor, now a free man, attended the theatre every night to applaud his saviour. Respectable citizens stayed away but, when my engagement was announced, every box was once again taken and crowds assembled at the pit and gallery doors. I was thrilled by the thought of a dead man restored to life like Earl Reginald in *The Castle Spectre*, but Mama was horrified by the prospect of encountering the miscreant, which strengthened her desire to escape 'this benighted island'. So she raised no objections – at least none that either I recall or the chroniclers record – when Papa accepted a proposal from Mr Jackson, the manager of the Glasgow and Edinburgh theatres, for me to perform in both cities in May.

We prepared to cross the sea for the first time in six years, but the voyage was delayed on account of Mama's 'interesting condition'. Unversed in such circumlocutions, I failed to see anything interesting in lying in bed and vomiting, especially since, when we finally set sail, the rough sea rendered us all bilious.

We embarked at Port Patrick on the next stage of my theatrical progress. With the new country came a new name. Although I had been dubbed The Young Roscius in Ireland, it was in Scotland that the name gained currency. Greeting us at Drury Lane, Mr Sheridan, who regularly spoke in riddles, felicitated Mr Hough, who was less gratified by the compliment than I expected: 'The Young Roscius' reputation soars before him. Were I to write *The Critic* now, I should add another puff to my character's catalogue: the puff infantile, in which I perceive that you are an adept.'

When I first saw the appellation on a bill, I knew nothing of Roscius, and learning that he was an actor in the Rome of Julius Caesar left me little the wiser. Why should anyone wish to associate me with a man who had died nearly two thousand years earlier? But the association was with one who had died far more recently: David Garrick, the English Roscius and Mr Hough's idol. In his view, the stage had mouldered since Garrick's death, under the sway of Mr Kemble and his followers. Now a new champion had entered the lists: a Child of Nature, whose very youth was enough to exempt him from Mr Kemble's purported pedantry. The public was set to encounter Garrick reborn.

3

One question above all gnaws at my brain. Was I a prodigy equipped by Nature to play characters of every stamp, or a youth of rare ability who would come into my own when I was of age, my heart more conversant and figure more congruent with the passions I portrayed? If the former, I may already have attained my meridian; if the latter, my second incarnation will transcend my first.

The question was much debated during my early renown, with many of my most fervent admirers entreating Papa to withdraw me from the stage for a period, in order that I might gain the grounding in the classics necessary both to crown my performances and permit me to take my place in the first society. Papa, sensible of the pain such a rupture would cause me, protested. Where else would I obtain such knowledge of the world as by appearing in the work of the most august authors? Where else would I have occasion to discover, let alone articulate, such profound and polished thought?

Papa's argument prevailed, but there was a part of me that would have welcomed being sent away to school. In that, I was guided by my one boyhood friend (that is the one friend of my own age), William Macready, with whom I am presently to renew my acquaintance.

I was a solitary child. In Ballynahinch, Mama proscribed all intercourse with the village boys, and my intimacy with our neighbours, the Rawdon children at Montalto, was sundered when Lord Moira, heartbroken by the treachery of his tenants during the Rebellion, sold the estate. Such fellowship as I enjoyed was with adults: Mama, of course, and Papa, when he was not occupied with affairs, and the cook and maids and groom and gardeners at Springhill, which, on reflection, must have stood me in good stead when I was thrown into the company of players. So I was delighted when Mr Macready, the manager of the Birmingham theatre, introduced me to his son, who was home from Rugby school. A year or so younger than me, he became my playmate both then and during my subsequent engagements, once even taking French leave to see me perform in Leicester. He told me thrilling tales of his antics at school and led me in adventures of our own, as we escaped our elders in the hidden crannies of the theatre, scaling ladders to the fly galleries and racing across the bridges between the side-wings. He was the one who was punished – and, as I recall, beaten – for his foolery, but he said that it was worth any number of stripes to hear the gasps of horror when I feigned a fall.

I was spared the rod but not the remonstrances of Papa, who charged me with both risking my neck and selfishness (a strange and, one might think, inconsistent combination), nor of Mr Hough, who charged me with puerility (an equally incongruous indictment of a twelve-year-old boy).

Macready is much in my thoughts as I ride to Wolverhampton, where I am to play for two nights and he comes as emissary from his father to discuss terms for my performances in Birmingham. It was on this same journey eight years ago that villagers lined the roads to watch my carriage pass, for all the world as if I were Lord Nelson after his victory at the Nile. At the time I was perplexed by the devotion of people who had never seen me act; now I admit to a tinge of regret that the only witnesses are an indifferent carter and shepherd. I meet with a similar reception in town where, having enquired the way to the Bell Inn from a surly constable, I relinquish my gig to an ostler, whose deferential smile is prompted purely by the prospect of emolument. I enter the inn and give my name to the housekeeper, who informs me that a gentleman attends me in the coffee room. She leads me to the door, where I spy Macready by the fire, resting his elbow on the chimney-piece. It is six years since last we met and he too has reached man's estate, but I remark at once the wide brow, strong chin, drooping mouth and crooked nose, which, as he gratefully acknowledged, would never find favour on the stage. I walk towards him, only to realise with dismay that he has failed to recognise me. Bowing quickly, I mumble an excuse about seeing to the horses and hurry away, promising to return.

A dour servant escorts me to my bedchamber, where I wash off the grime but not the disappointment. I tell myself that, while Macready's youthful image may be fixed in my memory, mine is stamped on prints and miniatures, plates and boxes, brooches and fans, and is therefore harder to dislodge. But I fear that it is my figure, not my face, that confounds him. The elfin grace that was so much admired is concealed – or rather, protected – by a layer of flesh. Now when they cheer, I can be sure that it is for my artistry and not my appearance. Where is it written that Norval or Selim or Tancred or Vasa or Richard or even Romeo is thin? Hamlet, we know, is fat, since Gertrude, who would surely have spared his sensibilities, describes him so during his duel with Laertes. Mr Hough required all my stage mothers to amend the word to *faint*. At last I can be truthful to the text.

I return to the coffee room to find Macready seated at a table. Eager to redress any brusqueness in my previous manner, I advance on him with an outstretched arm. He stands and, after a momentary pause, takes it coolly.

'Excessive profusions of intimacy, Betty, are one of the faults of our degraded profession.'

I realise that I have now offended him twice over and that we are no longer to be on first-name terms. But I also hear an *our* when I expected a *your* and, as I dispatch the servant for a bowl of rum punch, I express my surprise.

'I thought that you were to be a lawyer . . . Lord Chancellor, if I remember rightly.'

'You do indeed,' he replies, leading me to wonder why I should recall the particulars of his life better than my own. 'I was obliged to trade the wig and gown for the sock and buskin, when my father's affairs floundered and I quit school. My dreams of Oxford vanished, as if the courts and spires had been painted on flat-scenes which trundled off the stage. At sixteen, I had to take over my father's companies in Chester and Newcastle. He was . . . indisposed.'

'I am so sorry. To leave Rugby and all the japes with which you regaled me. How I envied you!'

'You envied me!' His face breaks into a smile. 'There was not a boy in the land who did not envy the celebrated Master Betty. My credit with my schoolfellows soared when they learnt of our association.'

'Association? No, friendship! You are my friend, William.' I try the name tentatively.

'I used to have so many friends. No longer. I will not discomfit them by parading my misfortune. If I am to recover their friendship, I have to earn it. Other professions confer on one the rank of gentleman, but a player can obtain it only by merit.'

'You are too harsh on yourself . . . on us all. I was received in the greatest houses – indeed, palaces.'

'Master Betty was a phenomenon. The rest of us are held in lower regard. The audience both revere and resent us for the passions we make them feel: passions so much greater than those that they feel in their own lives. They reckon that they have paid their dues when they buy their checks and, after that, we are fair game. I have seen young bucks climb up from the pit to rescue Rolla, when they considered him to be unjustly confined. I have witnessed their unmannerly conduct to the actresses, treating them as if they were no better than the strumpets who haunt the alleyways outside. Yet were I to leap to their defence, they would disdain to fight me because I am not their equal.'

Some men might welcome their freedom from such perilous encounters, but it is evident that the dishonour cuts him to the quick. I wonder whether his acute affectability is a help or a hindrance to his playing. I ladle him another cup of punch, which he drains in one.

'Had my mother lived, matters would have been very different. She would never have permitted my father to sink into debt . . . But I am forgetting that you also had to contend with an improvident father.'

'Oh no, William,' I say sternly. 'You are mistaken. I admit that the war had caused my father temporary embarrassment. The disruption of trade and the duties imposed on the linen he exported to the Indies had depleted his coffers. But he did not look to me to replenish them. He was persuaded that I had a rare talent and it would have been wrong to deny me the chance to exercise it. For all that, he was reluctant to let me perform but, once the venture was launched, he pursued it with vigour.'

'I have no wish to offend you, Betty, but his gallantries and his gaming were public knowledge.'

'I trust that my judgement of my own father will prevail over the fabrications of tattlers and hacks.'

'Yes, of course. If you say so.'

Even as he responds, in a tone that bespeaks courtesy rather than conviction, I hear Papa's voice ringing in my ears. I see myself slumped in a chair, as he rubs alcohol on my arms and legs to revive me in the interact, like a groom cooling down a horse after a race. 'Rouse yourself, William! It is your entrance. You must return to the stage. I beseech you! If they cancel your engagement, we shall all be ruined. Mama and Marianne will have nowhere to lay their heads. Do not think badly of me! A man can have ill luck at the faro table. As for women, you will find that they cost you dear!'

I muffle his voice and turn back to Macready. 'If my father were so improvident, how comes it that I am in possession of a fine estate, with revenues to provide for my mother and my sister for life?'

'In that case, I ask more urgently than ever: why, if there is no necessity, do you subject yourself to further buffets? You are no fairground pugilist, with torn ears and blackened eyes, who staggers up at the count of nine, desperate for the purse.'

'What buffets? It is true that there were critics who professed me too young for my characters – although was it more discrepant that I should play Norval, Selim or Hamlet at thirteen than that Mr Kemble should play them at fifty? I grant too that there were certain inopportune moments. I still hear the laughter when, as the Scottish king, I trembled to see Banquo's ghost and Mrs Powell asked me if I were a man. But those were incidentals, lines that Mr Hough, who was otherwise so diligent, should have excised. They were outweighed a hundredfold by the tokens of esteem I received nightly: on the stage; in my dressing room . . .' My throat suddenly feels dry. 'I am told, by those more studied in such matters than I, that no actor – not even Garrick himself – has ever been so favoured.'

'I well believe it. I shall never forget the frenzy that greeted you in Birmingham. Then, after you left us, we read of your reception elsewhere. How they rang the church bells in Sheffield – was it Sheffield? – when you agreed to give an extra performance! How the whole country went Roscius mad! And that was just a prelude to your triumphs in London. But I would not be your friend if I failed to remind you of the sequel, when the town turned against you.'

'With respect, William, you are mistaken. You have heeded the same common bruit about me as about my father. I cannot blame you. For far too long I myself subscribed to such falsehoods. Then last week, I finally remembered the truth. It was as though the mists had cleared . . . no, the mists remain, but familiar figures may be discerned within them. So many eminent personages, led by the Prince of Wales, had expressed concern about my health . . . no, my education . . . no, both. The passions I exhibited on the stage, the parties I attended off it, had taken their toll. My father bowed to their entreaties to remove me from the profession until I had the strength both of mind and of body to deal with its demands.'

'So you chose to quit?'

'Indeed.'

'Forgive me, I must have misconstrued. And yet—'

'We shall say no more about it.' I am so glad to hear him admit the error that, brushing aside his demurral, I order another bowl of the punch. 'You question my need to return, but I do so not merely for myself; I owe it to all those who were zealous in my cause. I am no choir-boy whose quality vanished when his voice cracked, but a player who has grown in experience and understanding. I am all that I was and more. Much more.' I pat my stomach to show him that I feel no unease about my girth.

'You have patently . . . expanded,' he says, with a smile. 'It is not for me to dissuade you from the undertaking if your heart is set on it.'

'It is.'

'I have no doubt that there will be crowds to cheer you on. My father certainly counts upon it. He has not sent me here out of sentiment. I for one will be pleased to reacquaint myself with Master—'

'Mister.'

'Betty. Although I was a schoolboy and green in judgement, I have known nothing to match the thrill of your performances: Selim; Fredrick; even the more manly roles of Richard and Osmond.'

'You are most kind,' I say, fearful of betraying my emotion.

'Although for me the nonpareil was Norval.'

For once I do not resent the preference and declaim the familiar couplet:

'"My name is Norval; on the Grampian Hills
My father feeds his flocks."'
To my surprise, he picks up the thread:
'"A frugal swain,
Whose constant cares were to increase his store.
And keep his only son, myself, at home."' He blushes
when his rendition, pitched louder than mine, receives a
smattering of applause from a pair of dice players in the
inglenook. I, meanwhile, am proud that my performance
so stirred him that he recollects the lines several years on.

'I played the role myself last year in Newcastle,' he says,
lowering his eyes.

'You did?' I ask, mortified by my presumption. 'Splendid!'

'The Lady Randolph was Mrs Siddons.'

'In Newcastle?'

'She was journeying to make her farewell in Edinburgh and
had engaged to appear there for two nights along the way.'

'I yearned to act with her ever since I saw her in Belfast.
But she had a lumbago of the back that kept her from the
stage during both my London seasons . . . Norval opposite
Mrs Siddons! You lucky dog! Surely that has reconciled you
to the profession?'

'She was long past her peak. The loss of several front
teeth had made her whistly. She had grown stout and
required her Anna and a gentlewoman to raise her from
the ground. But, though her legs were weak, her attitudes
were more expressive than ever. Each look . . . each gesture
was sublime. I recall – no, I still feel – her fingers twining
my hair, when I knelt before her on learning that she was
my mother. I still hear the heartrending laugh and shriek,
when my death drove her into madness and she ran out to
fling herself from the precipice.'

'I had almost forgotten that such was Lady Randolph's end. I saw it enacted but once, when I first played the role in Belfast. Thenceforth, they dropped the curtain at my death, since the audience would not permit the performance to continue.'

'Which is much to their discredit.'

'It was a tribute.'

'To you, I grant. And do not misunderstand me; you deserved it. I never saw a Norval die so nobly. Would that I were possessed of such grace! Nevertheless, to truncate the play at its climax is a gross discourtesy to the rest of the cast, to say nothing of the author, whose denouement is destroyed.'

I serve us both more punch, which loosens our tongues and sweetens our memories, as we relive our youthful amity like two old stagers on the Covent Garden free list. All at once, he bangs his fist on the table and turns to the matter in hand. His father is offering me an engagement of eight nights, with the receipts equally apportioned, plus one night gratis for him and a benefit for me. I am content to take him at his (slightly slurred) word when he declares that these are the same terms I enjoyed in the past, since it signals his father's abiding faith in me. His already flushed face flushes redder when he avows that he hopes to have the pleasure of acting opposite me. I immediately propose *The Earl of Warwick* and *The Royal Oak*, both of which he approves, deferring to me in my choice of roles (Warwick and King Charles). He regrets that he will be unable to stay for my Tancred on the morrow, since he has to return to Birmingham to play Selim in *Barbarossa*, a title that he endows with two extra syllables and an extended sibilance. We part, after toasting our future association with another cup of punch.

My crapulence the following morning is a small price to pay for the renewal of such a valued friendship. Fresh air and cabbage water clear my head, and I play Tancred to my own satisfaction and that of a select house, in despite of a black-toothed and slavering Siffredi.

The next day I revisit another old friend, albeit one I must embody myself, when I play Osman for the first time in six years. The reunion is felicitous and sets me in good spirits for the continuation of my progress to Banbury, Gloucester, Worcester and Stroud. As the coach approaches the final destination, I feel a queasiness, which at first I associate with the odours emanating from the dissenting minister with the grubby preaching bands squeezed beside me, but then a memory returns of my previous visit here in 1808, shortly before I quit the stage. The theatre's leading actor, one Kean by name (although not, it transpired, by nature), who was due to play Laertes to my Hamlet and Glenalvon to my Norval, absconded on the eve of my arrival. His aberrant behaviour was as much remarked in the town as his mimetic power, and at first no one paid it any heed. The flustered manager insisted that he was so overawed by the prospect of acting alongside me that he had fled, although one of the actresses spitefully (but, doubtless, truthfully) reported that he had refused to 'play second fiddle to the puffed-up boy with the girl's name.'

By then I was inured to such calumnies and performed opposite his double, who fed me my cues and did not impede my points, which was all that I required. This Kean failed to appear for the rest of my stay and, while most of his fellows, weary of his waywardness, opined that he would be lying drunken in a ditch, a few more charitable souls expressed concern. I later learnt that he had spent all three days encamped in the woods, living on wild berries. I wonder with some trepidation whether he remains in the company and, if so, whether he will take flight again. But when, having refreshed myself at the inn and proceeded to the theatre, I broach the subject to the manager, he assures me that Kean left that same season to try his fortune on the Swansea circuit. He was last heard of in Exeter. It is as close as he will ever come to attaining his dream of a London engagement, since what his talent merits, his temperament denies.

Any sadness I might feel at my fall from favour vanishes at the thought of this *village Kemble*. I play with redoubled power and receive more huzzahs (albeit muted by the cramped auditorium) than at any performance since Bath.

From Stroud I return to Pyms Farm, where Mama's disapproval of my enterprise is exacerbated by the fleas which, in despite of fervent scrubbing and powdering, I have transported from the various inns along the way. Not only does she insist on my relinquishing all my habiliments to be scrubbed in vinegar, but she obliges me to wear my grandmother's old flea trap around my neck, more as a penance than a prophylactic. Finally, having washed, changed and offered myself for inspection like an orphan in a workhouse, I lead Marianne into the woods for a spirited account of my adventures. We return for dinner, where, making no mention of theatres, actors or audiences, Mama enquires about the various beauty spots and landmarks I visited, as if I had been on a sketching trip.

Two weeks later, with her prayers if not her blessing, I leave for Birmingham. Once again I relinquish my gig for the mail and the privacy of my reflections for the companionship of my fellow travellers. Cloaked in anonymity, I listen to the stories of a postmaster who has invented a kite to convey explosive devices across the Channel; a rector, intent on reforming the alphabet in accordance with its pronunciation; and a mournful girl soon to set sail for India to keep house for her widowed uncle. No one seeks to question me and I am happy to let others take the centre of the stage (I smile at the inadvertent pun). After bidding them farewell at the Old Crown, I make my way to the theatre to be greeted by both Macreadys. The elder moves towards me with the outstretched arm that his son has deemed overly familiar, his round face beaming with bonhomie.

'Master Betty! How good it is to see you!'

'It is Mister Betty now, Father,' his son says, sensible of my grimace.

'Of course, of course, but he will always be Master Betty to those who knew him in his prime.

"A little child, an angel fair
Graced with the Muses' fire,
A prodigy beyond compare
His country to inspire."'

I am startled, as he recites a celebratory ode that I had long forgotten. His own memory stalling at the first quatrain, he seeks to conceal the lapse in a flurry of chatter. 'It does me good to see you once again, sir. How was your journey? Are you well quartered at the Crown? Should you want for anything, please do not hesitate to ask and we will do our utmost to oblige. Your friends here – and you still have many – would not wish for Master . . . Mister Betty to be in any way incommoded. How many years is it now? Six? Seven? You will find the theatre little changed.'

'Enough, Father! Give Mr Betty a chance to draw breath.'

'Of course. Loquacity was ever my undoing. Forgive me,

sir. It is fruitless to crave pardon from my son. But he is more than my son; he is my right arm, my mainstay, my fidus Achates.'

'Father . . .'

'I know: loquacity! At sixteen, he took charge of my company when, harried by my creditors, I was arraigned for debt and mewed up in the bowels of Lancaster Gaol.' I look away from Macready, who reddens with both shame and fury as I apprehend the full extent of his father's *indisposition*. 'He provided for one who should have provided for him, but Nature has so contrived that we may not choose our fathers.' I nod, as eager as his son to bring the colloquy to an end. 'But may I enquire after the health of Mr Betty . . . Mr Betty senior, that is?'

'You may, but not I fear of me,' I reply, in an effort to lighten the mood. 'My father has been dead for almost a year.'

'My condolences. I had not heard. Why did you not tell me?' He turns a pained gaze on his son. 'He was not always easy or gracious or kind but, if I may quote the melancholy Dane: "He was a man, take him for all in all, I shall not look upon his like again."' Macready raps his knuckles on the desk, a remonstrance to which his father is either oblivious or indifferent. 'He had his son's best interests at heart, although he did not always know how best to advance them. He was never fully conversant in the ways of the theatre. His cardinal error was to dismiss Mr Hough.'

'Father, I am quite sure that Mr Betty does not wish to rake over old coals.'

'Oh but I do,' I reply, in a mild rebuke to my friend. 'There is so much that I have forgotten . . . so much more that I never knew.'

'I have met many who were adept at beating the drum,

but none with the proficiency of Mr Hough. He saw that the public longed for the glory days of Garrick. They were bored with the stateliness of Mr Kemble.'

'He likened him once to the statue who came to life in *The Libertine*,' I say, with a pang of unease.

'That is unjust,' Macready interjects, unable to hide his resentment of my rapport with his father.

'No doubt, no doubt,' Mr Macready says. 'But was it not Mr Sheridan who suggested playing music during his pauses?' Macready makes no reply. 'Mr Hough puffed you as the new Garrick, a Child of Nature. Of course, when your father dismissed him, he recanted and claimed to have taught you everything you knew. He brought out another boy. I forget his name. I journeyed to see him in Hull. He spoke with a thick Scottish accent and a lisp.'

A wave of melancholy sweeps over me as I recall my tutor's voice. *You are unique. There has never been another actor like you. Even Garrick began life as a wine merchant. Your school – your nursery – is the stage.*

'So you did not engage him?'

'Not all the puffery and ringers in the world could have commended him to the public. He was no Master Betty.'

My fixed smile fails to deceive Macready, who finally extricates me from his father. Although there are three days until *The Royal Oak* opens, he is eager to rehearse.

The company awaits me in the green room and, as in Bath and Stroud, several of them allude to our prior acquaintance. I do my best to confirm their reminiscences and am relieved to find them so fond. I had feared that my fellow players would have resented my renown and thought me conceited. On the contrary, they vie to praise my modesty.

One, Mrs Holmes (then Miss Davies), recollects how I promised to perform for her and Mr Holmes' benefit (a promise she admits that she secured in the side-wing, knowing full well that I had no authority to grant it). Papa was furious and, in despite of my tearful pleas, refused to let me appear, whereupon I offered to call on all the first families to elicit support. As a result, the pair enjoyed the most remunerative night of their lives, with receipts of a hundred and sixty-two pounds. 'And eighty-eight pence,' her husband adds, as if to acknowledge every farthing of their debt. I dimly recall such a round of visits but had thought that it had been with Mama, taking Christmas viands to Papa's spinners in Ballynahinch. I am delighted to discover that my youthful merits were not confined to the stage.

Macready is impatient to proceed and he escorts me to the stage, where Mr Bartley, the prompter, defers to him as the manager's son as much as to me, the visiting auxiliary. We start by rehearsing the business, which is unusually protracted since I have various entrances within the scenes: from the mouth of the royal tent on my first appearance; along the rockface on my last; and, at particular hazard to my person, descending from the titular tree during the storm. The steps behind the foliage creak ominously, and Mr Bartley assures me both that the sound will be drowned by the roll of the thunder-trunk and the planks will be reinforced. Noting my abashment, he adds that Mr Courtney, for whom they were made, is of cadaverous build.

As if the presence of our fellow actors offers him a licence that he would not enjoy in a tête-à-tête, Macready asserts that no actor can afford to become portly. 'Would an artist paint on an unstretched canvas or a fiddler play on a loosened string?' He smiles as though to divest the words of offence, and I smile back as though to show that I have taken none, but the ensuing silence attests to the general discomfiture. What he says may well be true, but then he is not a man whose talent will ever be obscured by his beauty.

We conclude the business with my boarding the ship that is to conduct me to safety in France and which, Mr Bartley informs me, will traverse the back of the stage, an effect far beyond the scope of the carpenters when I performed the piece in Worcester. We then turn to the speeches and the songs, of which there are many: ballads for Claribel and choruses for the soldiers but, to my regret, nothing for the king.

Some of the cast, although well practised in their roles, fumble for words, to Macready's visible and at times audible annoyance, but I, who have played King Charles only twice, find that the facility for memorising lines, which had served me so well in my nonage, has not deserted me. I am mightily relieved since, contrary to custom, Macready rehearses at the height of his powers and I find myself driven to respond, until we might be playing to a packed house and not a small band of our compeers, who nonetheless give us several rousing hands.

Three days later, the house is, indeed, packed to suffocation. Visiting me in my room before the curtain, Mr Macready cannot contain his delight. 'The name of Betty is still a draw in Birmingham,' he avows, which should come as no surprise when there is not a single *Mr* to be seen on a playbill, as if I were truly a prodigy of Nature, who has returned from a five-year absence without ageing a day. The audience reward me with a burst of applause on my entrance and again when I rebut Cromwell's envoy,

Lambton, defying the so-called Protector's usurping power and declaring myself 'a duteous and a loving son to England.' Later, an even louder burst greets my refusal to regain my throne with 'aid from vaunting France.' Although with Buonaparte's forces ranged against us, the sentiment would doubtless be commended irrespective of the speaker.

I am conscious of the excellence of Macready's playing, which more than offsets the defects of his person. I cannot pretend that the warmth of his reception derives solely from his being a local favourite. I trust that I am not one to begrudge a fellow actor's success, but then I have never before had occasion to do so. In despite of my best intentions, my playing grows listless. Macready remarks it and, when the company retires to the tavern after the performance, he draws me aside.

'I hope that you will not take umbrage if I speak my mind, Betty.'

'No, of course, my dear fellow,' I say, lifting my tankard to my lips as a first line of defence.

'You did not do yourself justice tonight. Where was the passion – the power – I saw in rehearsal? I am used to complaining about actors who reserve their efforts for the performance but, in your case, the opposite holds true.'

'I accept the reproof, but I beg you to understand how hard it is for me when the audience are cold.'

'Tepid at worst.'

'Tepid is cold to one whose every word – every gesture – was once greeted with acclaim. The plaudits I received on the delivery of my great speeches not only offered welcome affirmation of the audience's approval but enabled me to recover my breath and prepare my effects.'

'Which is why you must win them round. You must play

with the same passion when there is one enthusiast in the house as when there are a thousand. That is what marks the adept from the dilettante.'

I take his words to heart and strive to give of my best for the remainder of my engagement, notwithstanding the depleted houses and muted huzzahs. Macready appears satisfied and we part as friends, promising a future association to include Romeo and Mercutio, Pierre and Jaffier, even Othello and Iago, at Covent Garden or Drury Lane.

Eight years ago it might have been at both, for it was in Birmingham that preparations were made for my London debut. For once I cannot blame any confusion on my defective memory, since I was not a party to negotiations. Of course I recall that Mr Kemble made the journey to see me, but I only have Mr Holmes' word that he coughed throughout the performance. Even so, I refute the imputation that he was seeking to distract me. He suffered from asthma, which was especially severe during the seasons of 1805 and 1806 and which, like his sister Mrs Siddons' lumbago, prevented our sharing the stage.

Given that his visit was unauthorised, he very properly refrained from felicitating me, but he must have reported favourably on my performance for, days later, an agent arrived from Covent Garden, hotly pursued by one from Drury Lane. Papa conferred with them both, before settling on Covent Garden. The terms, for whose details I have to thank the memoirists, were the most generous ever offered to any player, regardless of age: fifty guineas a night for twelve performances and a benefit free of all charges. Mr Hough, whose aversion to Mr Kemble was no longer confined to his acting, crowed that 'Kemble only takes thirty-seven pounds ten shillings a week.'

His jubilation was short-lived, for Mr Sheridan, fearing the losses that would accrue to his theatre from my engagement by his rival, combined with those who, solicitous of my welfare, sought my removal from the stage. Papa was incensed, accusing the noble author of *Pizarro* of every species of treachery. Then either Mr Sheridan himself or someone serving his interests discovered that, although I was contracted to Covent Garden for certain nights, there was nothing but convention to keep me from playing at Drury Lane on the others. I would be the first player in anyone's remembrance – perhaps in history – to be employed by both houses at once. Mr Hough remonstrated that I would find the exertion too fatiguing and, had she not been recuperating in Edinburgh after the birth of Marianne, I suspect that Mama would have concurred, but Papa insisted that it was an honour that only an ingrate churl – or worse, an Irish rebel – would refuse.

These days I would give my left arm (my right, I recall wryly, is required to make my points) for an offer from either house, but, although Mr Macready has written to both Covent Garden and Drury Lane on my behalf, neither has seen fit to send representatives. I have more success with the country managers and, after a restful sojourn at Pyms Farm, where my reports – duly embellished – of my reception in Birmingham serve to reconcile Mama to my enterprise, I set off on the next stage of my travels: to Manchester, Sheffield, Leicester and Liverpool.

As I scan the memoirs for accounts of my previous visits to these mercantile cities, I fear that I will resemble Marianne scouring the *Salopian Journal* for notice of her attendance at the Lloyd's Patriotic Fund annual picnic. But, when my adult performances meet with at best indifference and at worst derision, I wish to remind myself of how my arrival in Manchester, 'a town dedicated to commerce, which had hitherto displayed little interest in the mimetic arts,' was greeted by bands and banners; how, in Sheffield, I 'melted the hearts of the men of steel' and my 'playing proved to be keener than the sharpest blade'; and how, in Leicester, in order to appease disappointed patrons, I took the unprecedented step of giving both a morning and evening performance on the same day.

This time, the disappointment is mine, when not even Norval can command a full house. After a week blighted by sleeplessness, I am eager to arrive refreshed in Liverpool. So, on the eve of my departure, I take a calming draught of Dover's Powder, only to wake at ten to find that I have missed the coach. Bleary-eyed, I hire a gig to Derby and then a post-chaise to Chester. I dine at haste before boarding the mail for Liverpool, in which I am writing these lines – much to the irritation of my neighbour, who shuffles in his seat as though to intimate that, with my table on my knees, I am taking up more than my allotted space. The occupation soothes my nerves, which have been frayed ever since I spotted a blunderbuss poking from beneath the postillion's box-coat.

Enjoining me not to alarm my fellow passengers, he reported several recent attacks from tobymen on Tranmere Hill. My fears are confirmed when, no sooner do we reach the hill than we come to an abrupt halt. I grab my inkpot before it causes my neighbour a genuine grievance and smile reassuringly at the young lady opposite who, mistaking my intentions, flutters both her eyelashes and her fan. To my relief, the obstruction is arboreal and, once it has been removed, we proceed without further ado. After taking the Woodside Ferry, we arrive at the Talbot Inn where, deeming that the trials of the journey license me to defy Macready's injunction, I order a substantial supper of cold meats, collops and eggs, rice pudding and gooseberry pie.

There is a certain melancholy surrounding a town whose fortune was founded on the sale of our fellow mortals, a fact of which I remained in blissful ignorance during my previous visit. On that occasion, my chief concerns were my first sighting of my infant sister, Marianne, whom Mama, freed from her lying-in, brought to join us, and my first brush with a member of that exalted family, which was to take such a gracious interest in my progress. This was Prince William Frederick of Gloucester, Military Commander of the North West district, who invited Papa and me to dine at his private villa, and requested that I play his dukedom's most notorious antecedent, Richard III.

An admonitory look from Papa secured my assent, although the Crookback was never one of my favoured characters. Not only was I closer in age to the hapless princes, but Mr Hough refused to allow me to wear a hump. He had decried the Belfast players, who barely varied their appearance between roles, yet my Richard looked little different from my Hamlet.

As ever, he had a rejoinder to my misgivings and, as ever, it lay in my face.

'Your youthful beauty makes his plight even more cruel. Like other men who have been told by their supposed superiors that they are unsuited to their chosen paths in life, he has adopted their opinions as his own. If his nature has been warped, it is by their jibes, their taunts, their unjust dismissals. Even his own mother wishes that she had never borne him. How would you feel if Mrs Betty said such a wicked thing to you?'

'Sad.'

'No, you would feel embittered! Full of hatred. You would seek revenge and, like Richard, you would stop at nothing to achieve it. You would show yourself worthy of the crown by your strategies, even as you showed yourself unworthy by your crimes.'

I adhered to his prescript and the prince declared himself delighted by my rendition. He held a reception in my honour, attended by all the quality in the region.

'Let me introduce you to my friend, Thomas Lister Parker, Bowbearer of the Forest of Bowland. Parker, this is—'

'But he needs no introduction. The whole world resounds with his fame. Albion's glory! A lad unparalleled! I kiss your hand.' I blushed as he lifted it to his lips, his own hand as cold and clammy as a cellar wall. 'Your humblest, most devoted servant.'

'Rum cove!' the prince remarked affectionately. I snatched back my hand, but the kiss was imprinted on my skin – and my memory.

Papa did not share my qualms, accepting the Bowbearer's invitation to escort me to Browsholme Hall, his house in the heart of the Ribble Valley. Our host took great pride in showing us the collection of drawings and mezzotints that he had brought back from France during the temporary lull in hostilities two years before. One, which he claimed to have made himself, depicted a boy with thick, tow-coloured hair, who clasped the wing of an eagle that was transporting him through the sky.

'This should be of especial interest to you, William,'

he said. Mindful that I was his guest, I set aside the far more interesting print of The Execution of King Lewis XVI. 'I copied it from the ceiling of the Villa Farnesina in Rome. *The Rape of Ganymede* or, as I entitle it, *Ganymede Transcendent.*'

'He looks about to slide off.'

'Have no fear, he is safe in the clutches of Zeus. Do you know the story?'

'I know Zeus,' I replied, loath to be lectured outside of a rehearsal.

'Has he not studied Homer?' the Bowbearer asked Papa.

'You must enquire of my wife,' Papa said, with a deprecatory shrug. 'She resisted all my attempts to send him to school. She would have him ever by her side.'

'And who can blame her?' the Bowbearer replied, before addressing me. 'In brief, Zeus, king of the gods, lays eyes on Ganymede, a Trojan prince, tending his flocks on Mount Ida. Homer describes Ganymede as "the fairest of all that breathed," although there can be no question but that he would revise that verdict were he writing today.' He turned to Papa. 'Do you not agree?'

'I am no poet.'

'No. Zeus thought the boy so beauteous that, forsaking his usual run of amours, he transformed himself into an eagle and carried him off to Olympus, where he made him immortal. What do you say to that, William?'

'I would like to be immortal.'

'Trust me, you shall be. But I have a device in mind to redouble your glory. It is so perfect that I can hardly bring myself to speak it out loud.'

'Steel yourself, sir,' Papa said, and the Bowbearer, ignorant of his humour, took him at his word.

'What if I were to bespeak a drama on the legend from, say, Mr Colman or Mr Cumberland? It would be William's greatest role – greater even than Norval, one which would exhibit all his genius . . . all his charms.'

'Would I have to fly?' I asked, disturbed by the prospect of the jolting machinery.

'You would soar!'

'Is there matter enough in it?' Papa asked. 'The Young Roscius must have occasion for his points.'

'A plenitude. After the rape . . . that is the flight, Hera, Zeus' queen, with typical female malice, seeks revenge on his beloved. Meanwhile, the boy's aged tutors try to draw him back to Troy.'

'That would be Mr Hough,' I said, eager to acknowledge one who had been excluded from the festivities.

'Ah but they fail,' the Bowbearer said, with a sly smile. 'As all must in the face of a doting god.'

'What of the boy's father?' Papa asked. 'How does he sustain the loss of his son?'

'Rest assured, he is lavishly recompensed. In one account, Zeus gives him a team of immortal horses – but, even were we to commandeer Mr Astley's stable, that would be impracticable; in another, he gives him a golden vine. I think that that would satisfy any father. Do you not agree?'

I make my way to the theatre, where I introduce myself to my fellow actors. By now, I should not be surprised to find several who declare themselves veterans of my previous engagement, although they are less effusive in their welcome than their counterparts in Birmingham, Bath and Stroud. One is actively hostile.

'Charles Ainsworth,' he says stiffly. 'I do not expect you

to recall the face of one so lowly as I, but perhaps my back will jog your memory?' He wheels round with a flourish.

'He looks confounded,' a second seasoned player, Mr Hawtree, interjects. 'Here is Hamlet, Cato, Lusignan, a peerless actor whom you made your plaything, compelling him to stoop and let you leap over his shoulders before you would deign to step on to the stage.'

'I crave your pardon,' I say, cringing as I find myself the object of general disfavour. 'I was a boy: heartless, thoughtless, unrestrained.'

Mr Ainsworth snorts, while the rest of the company stay silent, and I have rarely been more grateful for the prompter's summons. The play is *The Castle Spectre* and Earl Osmond one of my best-loved roles, even though when I performed it at Covent Garden, there were many who considered it unseemly that I should play a murderous, licentious villain rather than the virtuous Percy.

'May I ask if we are permitted to touch Master Betty—'

'Mr Betty,' I interject feebly.

Although his principal has retired, Mr Hawtree maintains the assault. 'When he last graced us with his presence, we were subject to a strict edict to do so only when unavoidable. Woe betide anyone who upset our young sweeting!'

'That edict, as you put it, was not issued by me,' I reply, with all the dignity I can muster. 'Nor is there any such now. I am here to serve the play, just like you.'

'Very well. Now that the matter is settled, let us begin,' the prompter says.

I feel so despondent as we rehearse the business that I raise no objections when it conflicts with my habitual practice. Nothing cheers me, not even the appearance of the Spectre herself, an effect which, as the prompter points out, will be greatly enhanced by the new-fashioned reflectors on the oil lamps. The gloom persists when we turn to the speeches. My memory falters and I stammer and pause, no doubt earning further contempt from the cast.

Midway through the reading, when Mr Ainsworth as Father Philip steals into the castle hall, I remember why I humbled him. The offence was not mine but his. Entering the green room, I heard him demand that my gender be medically verified. My person, my performances and even my name were feminine. Moreover, the sentiments of the gentlemen in the pit could only be explained – indeed, justified – if the *he* were a *she*. Although as yet unaware of the full implication of the insult, I was outraged. Did he not know of the billets-doux I received from ladies of family, whose carnal proposals appalled Mama? Did he not know of the laundress who stole my undergarments and the actress who sneaked up behind me and snipped a lock of my hair? Had he not heard of the lady in Sheffield who stripped to her chemise while watching my Romeo and had to be forcibly restrained from joining me in the tomb?

Fired by my remembrance, I resume the rehearsal with new fervour which, although carried over into the performance, is not matched by the audience's response. I fear that I have found the answer to the question that has consumed me since I made my return in Bath, and, like Chatterton if not Mozart, I am one who reached the acme of my achievement in my youth. I retire to my dressing room and divest myself of the costume that mocks my hopes. The silence is so sombre that I think fondly of the crush that had once dismayed me. My longing for distraction is met by an emphatic knocking and, after pulling on my breeches and tucking in my shirt, I open the door to a man of about my own age, height and colouring. He enters and fixes me with a glower.

'Master Betty,' he says, after an awkward interval.

'It is Mr Betty now,' I say wearily.

'Ah, but I am Master Wilson.'

'Is this a puzzle?'

'Would that it were! Do you not recognise my name?'

'Forgive me, but I encountered so many people during my boyhood.' I take my clue from his accent. 'Was it in Scotland?'

'The Caledonian Roscius.'

'Indeed,' I reply, none the wiser.

'Although my fame, unlike yours, never reached further south than Sheffield. But we shared a dramatic tutor.'

'Mr Hough?'

'The same. Why do you look so shocked? Did you think that his ambitions died when your father dismissed him?'

'I have never given it much thought,' I reply. Although the truth is that I have never ceased to ponder it.

'No, why should you? He had helped you to attain your desire, but he desired so much else for himself. He had known my father when they were young.'

'In London?'

'No, Doncaster, Wakefield and Hull; on the Yorkshire circuit.'

'He would never speak of his acting days to me.'

'My father said that he was quite the worst actor he ever saw. He had all the dedication . . . all the discernment, but none of the facility. And when Mr Kemble, crowned with London laurels, came to York on his summer tour, he admonished him so severely that he never acted again.'

'No wonder that he felt so bitter towards him.'

'It is natural to feel bitter towards someone we blame for all our wrongs, but we will come to that later. When he parted from you, Mr Hough moved to Whitby, taking a room in my parents' lodging-house. He convinced them to let him prepare me for the stage. He swore that he could replicate the success he had enjoyed with you.'

'But your lisp . . .'

'Yes. Thank you for mentioning it. That did not deter him. On the contrary, the impediment seemed to encourage him: allowing him to show what he could fabric from the most unpromising material. If he carved you out of perfect marble, then I was marble with a flaw.'

'I should not have spoken. The lisp is barely audible.'

'You are making a cross for your own grave!' Startled, I wonder what he might be concealing under his coat and edge towards the property dagger on my chair. 'Unlike you, I never wished to act. We all know "I shall surely die if I may not be a player!"' He quotes the remark that has been repeated to me so often that it no longer sounds like my own – if, indeed, it ever was. 'I failed abjectly and was hissed off the stage.'

'You have every right to blame him.'

'When did I say that? The person I blame is you.' I am horrified and wait for him to explain. 'I feel sorry for him, still living in Whitby on the pension of fifty pounds a year from your father. Fifty pounds a year – a princely sum!'

'I was not privy to their terms.'

'No, you were too busy being fondled and caressed.'

'Cheered and acclaimed.'

'Such ingratitude!'

'That is a lie! I have always given him credit. He was the one who denied it. I studied hard and resented the suggestion that acting came as instinctually to me as breathing. But he insisted that no one wished to picture me drudging at a desk. The truth is that I was neither as immediate in my effects as my admirers would have it nor as schooled in them as my detractors maintained.'

'So you admit that you had detractors?'

'Some, yes. Then so did Mr Kemble. So even did Mrs Siddons.'

'But they were mere mortals, unlike you.'

'I must ask you to go. I wish to complete my toilet.'

'Surely you are accustomed to doing that under scrutiny? I shall not detain you long, but I have one further question. When he was discharged, Mr Hough declared that he would blazon his case abroad. My father showed me the notice in the newspaper. *An appeal to the sagacity and candour of the honourable British Public* or words to that effect. Then he withdrew his charge. He never published the promised correspondence with your father or the account of his methods with you. Why?'

'The reason is obvious. My father offered him the pension.'

'Fifty pounds a year, when you were earning as much in guineas every night! Why did he not hold out for more, unless he were afraid of your father's counter-charge?'

'What counter-charge? You are mistaken.'

'Remember who I am! Master Wilson. The Caledonian Roscius. I too came off the stage soaked in perspiration, to be rubbed down in private, the napkin – and the hand that held it – creeping slowly towards parts of me that remained dry.'

'Enough!'

'I too shared a chamber – and many unsought intimacies – with him, as we traversed the North.'

'I never shared a chamber with him. Not once!'

'After he had finished with me – after the world had finished with me – I was fit for nothing but to be a Marjorie or a Mary Ann.'

'Do you mean – ?'

'No. I am sorry if I disappoint you. I returned to school. I became the clerk to a notary in Chester. As a mark of his satisfaction, my master gave me an afternoon's leave to come here.'

'I am glad.'

'Are you in earnest?'

'Every syllable. You have shown me that I have nothing to fear from the past. Mr Hough respected me. He always said that I was unique and you have confirmed it.' *What a handsome boy!* 'He would rather have chopped off his hand than used it improperly towards me. Now you must go. My exertions have exhausted me. I wish to return to the hotel.'

4

I am returned to London and have taken up lodgings in Henrietta Street, a stone's throw from the Covent Garden theatre where, as today's *Morning Chronicle* informs me, *In compliance with the solicitations of several parties of distinction, the ci-devant Young Roscius is next Thursday to make his reappearance on the London stage.*

The revival of my fortunes is complete. Disheartened by my reception in the northern towns, I took refuge at Pyms Farm where Mama, assured of my abandoned ambition, berated the public who had failed to recognise such a nonpareil. Then on 13 September, when, to gratify Mama and Marianne, I was striving to take pleasure in the twenty-first birthday festivities they had devised for me, a missive arrived from Covent Garden offering me an engagement of twelve nights before Christmas and a further twelve thereafter. Moreover, it was to be on the same terms as my debut, viz fifty guineas per performance and two clear benefits. The sum is important, since it signals their confidence in my ability to draw – and to retain – an audience. Moreover, the letter was signed by my 'humble servant' (and, I trust, soon to be esteemed colleague), John Philip Kemble.

I am arrived three days in advance of rehearsal to reacquaint myself with the metropolis. I have taken a well-appointed, well-ventilated room, with my own pan closet, in a house run by a Mrs Stirling who, in despite of our brief acquaintance, has recounted a family history of such unrelenting tragedy that only Mrs Siddons could do it justice. From my window, I look across the piazza to Richardson's hotel, where I stayed on my first visit in December 1804. So many admirers assembled outside that a bear-tamer brought his dancing bear to entertain them, but I was not allowed to approach the window to see it for fear of provoking a stampede. My first notion was to put up there, but I have to remind myself as much as others that 'I am Mr Betty now.'

I walk out into the street and survey the scene, as though it were being enacted by supernumeraries at the nearby theatre, rather than extemporised by the crowd. I give sixpence to a boy soldier, his right sleeve pinned to his chest, who begs for alms, while a trio of apprentices playing at cudgels pays him no heed. I stroll through the piazza, unrecognised and unmolested save by three strumpets, identifiable by their red scarves and hitched-up skirts, who trail after me, hawking their wares. When I rebuke them for impudence, they whoop with laughter as if their sole purpose had been to goad me. Ruffled, I hurry down to the Strand, where I am further disconcerted by the sound of an elephant's trumpeting, until I see the sign for *Pidcock's Exotic Animals* on the second floor of the Exeter Exchange. I cross the road to the Italian Warehouse, where I buy four yards of pale blue damask for Mama and an ivory-and-swanskin fan for Marianne, trusting that the purchases will reconcile the one to my obduracy and the other to my absence. Resisting the lure of the strong-smelling cheeses and sausages ranged at the back of the store, I continue my progress towards Charing Cross, stopping to examine the display in a tailor's window. Before I have a chance to reflect, I have bought not only a new short-coat but a pair of trousers, a garment that the tailor assures me is no longer restricted to labourers and mariners but worn by gentlemen of the first fashion and, he lowers his voice discreetly, being looser than breeches, is more becoming to those of ample build. He gives me the name of Mrs Walcott, a seamstress in St Martin's Lane who can be trusted to shorten the legs. After calling on her, I make my way to Sawyer's to dine.

I am eager to attend the theatre and, although my loyalty to my new company does not preclude a visit to Drury Lane, where my old friend Mr Pope is appearing as Biron in *Isabella*, nothing can compare with the chance to see Mrs Jordan as Violante in *The Wonder*. Just as Mrs Siddons had inspired me with her lament for Elvira's lost innocence, so Mrs Jordan captivated me with her relish of Violante's assumed guilt. I saw the play only once, but I shall never forget the scene where, learning of her father's intent to dispatch her to a convent, her maid declared: 'To be sure, you look very like a nun.' With an expression at once saucy, surprised, even wistful, she enamoured the audience who, right down to the thirteen-year-old boy in the manager's box, knew her own history to be very different. She was the companion (I refuse to employ any harsher term) of the Duke of Clarence, to whom she had borne eight children, and not even a voluminous apron could disguise the fact that she was expecting a ninth.

At five o'clock, I make way across the piazza without undue haste, since I am promised that my name has been placed on the free list. I am keen to familiarize myself with the theatre, which has been entirely rebuilt since my last appearance. I recall Mr Sheridan exhorting me to savour my success since the materials of an actor's fame were perishable. In the event, he might have professed them *combustible*. Within six months of each other – a concurrence that solaced those of my colleagues at Christ's of an evangelical bent – both the Covent Garden and Drury Lane theatres burnt to the ground. While the former reopened within a year of the conflagration, the latter did so only two months ago and then without Mr Sheridan, whose removal was one of the conditions imposed by the building committee. Like his own Joseph Surface, Mr Sheridan, whose irregular finances were the despair of capital actors and the ruin of supernumeraries, has nowhere left to hide, and it is rumoured that he expects to be arraigned at any moment for debt. I pity him, even though he likened me to Carlo, the Newfoundland, whose dive to save a drowning infant had caused a sensation in 1803, and claimed that his theatre had been saved first by a dexterous dog and then by a golden goose.

Banishing such rueful remembrances, I reach the theatre's main entrance in Bow Street and gaze up at the elegant façade with its imposing portico and Grecian frieze, testament to Mr Kemble's classical aspirations. I proceed to Hart Street, where I give my name to the new box keeper.

'Master Betty, sir. Yes, I heard you was coming back.'

'It is Mr Betty now. Master Betty is one of the many ghosts buried in the rubble of the old building.' He looks bemused. 'I hoped to see Mr Brandon. Is he no longer with us?'

He appeared ancient to me six years ago, but then so did anybody over thirty.

'He is no longer with the theatre. Mr Kemble was obliged to dismiss him. A crying shame!' Now I must be looking bemused, for he takes it upon himself to elaborate. 'He had ordered the arrest of several of the ringleaders during the riots and they demanded his head as the price of peace. The O.P. riots, that is.'

'Yes, of course.'

The prolonged disturbances on the theatre's reopening, when agitators protested against the raised prices in the pit and boxes, were widely reported. For two months, they shouted and jeered, beat pans and shook rattles, fought, danced and ran races along the benches, threatening to wreak as much havoc as the flames. Even in Cambridge, where we were taught to emulate Christ's concern for those of humbler station, I felt no sympathy for this surge of theatrical Jacobinism. With the price of the one shilling gallery unchanged, it was pure devilry for its denizens to object to increases in parts of the house to which they would never gain admittance. Finally, Mr Kemble who, in his favoured role of Coriolanus, had so often capitulated to his mother to save his city, was compelled to do likewise to the mob to save his theatre.

Macready was right to bemoan the actor's lot. Audiences acclaim our impersonations while condemning us as impostors. They resent us for making wiser rulers, braver soldiers, more ardent lovers and truer friends than they. No doubt the women in Shakespeare's day begrudged the boys who made worthier mistresses, even as the men in our own day begrudged the boy who made a nobler hero.

I aim to put that boy behind me but, as I enter the auditorium, which to my indiscriminate eye appears little altered, he rushes past and takes his seat at the front of the box.

'Adagio, William!' Mr Hough cautions, as if I am hurtling through an expository speech, but we have only lately arrived in London and I am greedy for my first glimpse of the house. The pit and the galleries are packed, but the boxes are half-empty, although the play is about to start. We share our box with a hoary-headed gentleman who, Mr Hough whispers in my ear, is Mr Cumberland, author of *The Wheel of Fortune*, the evening's comedy. He greets my reverential smile with a gracious nod and betrays no annoyance at the empty seats. The curtain rises on the country cottage where Penruddock, played to my delight if not my tutor's by Mr Kemble, has retreated for twenty years after a disappointment in love. Even his admirers admit that Mr Kemble is not graced with gaiety, and his performance owes as much to Melpomene as to Thalia. Nevertheless, Mr Cumberland appears to be gratified by his effects, and I echo his laughter.

Wearied by the longueurs of the plot, I am diverted by the novelties of the stage, in particular the flat-scenes which, instead of sliding on and off in their grooves, are raised and lowered by pulleys. Lamps take the place of the candles in country theatres but, if the light is more focused, the stench is more noxious: burning oil smelling even fouler than melting tallow. As the boxes slowly fill during the second and third acts, I begin to understand Mr Cumberland's composure, but, to my horror if not his, the occupants salute one another as if they were at the races. The hushmen remonstrate in vain, and the intrigue in the house vies with that on the stage.

Unbeknownst to myself, I am a party to it. Midway through the fourth act, Mr Hough clasps my shoulder and commands me to stand. Wrenched from the world of the play, I blindly comply, while Mr Kemble, ignorant of the new distraction, speaks the line: 'Henry is young and, like the promise of a forward spring, flatters our hopes of harvest.' Immediately, voices ring out across the house. 'Look, the Young Roscius!'; 'I shall swoon'; 'He is even more beautiful than his picture'; 'How clever of them to present him here first to show that it is no mere trick of the light!' Meanwhile, a loud cry of 'He is a forward spring indeed and the token of a golden harvest' reveals that Mr Hough's timing was no accident.

'Bow,' he hisses in my ear.

'Why?' I say.

'They are applauding you.'

Squirming with embarrassment, I obey, exciting another flurry of flattery and applause. The next thing I know, a man is straddling the partition from the neighbouring box, and shouts and thuds in the passageway attest to a beleaguering crowd. With more persistence than agility, the intruder clambers over and, pushing Papa to one side, advances on me. A second man follows, with a third directly behind. Meanwhile, the door starts to crack, threatening imminent invasion. Mr Cumberland, observing my terror, hustles me through a door in the sidewall to the security of the manager's box. Shrugging off Papa's apologies, he returns to his seat to watch the remains of his play.

Papa and Mr Hough are exultant, but I am mortified. For the audience to treat me with such devotion – and Mr Kemble with such disrespect – is doubly unconscionable when I have yet to step out on the London stage. Do they set such store by reports from Sheffield and Birmingham, to which they have hitherto looked only for their cutlery and brass?

Mr Kemble makes no mention of the disruption when he greets me the next morning, insisting, to Mr Hough's marked irritation, that he pays no heed to occurrences in the house, a remark that perplexes me since I saw him nod to an acquaintance who hailed him from the pit. He escorts us to the green room, where he introduces us to Mr Farron, the prompter, who is to conduct the rehearsal of *Barbarossa*, before taking his leave.

'Will you not be attending?' Mr Hough asks.

'Alas, the duties of the acting manager are Sisyphean. Besides, there is nothing that I could impart to the innate genius of Master Betty,' he replies, which is gratifying but patently untrue. Feeling humbled by both Mr Kemble's generosity and my enrolment among the London players, I make my round of the green room, bowing to each of them in turn. Few attempt to conceal their curiosity about the youth of whose prowess they have received such intelligence, and I am grateful for Mr Hough's injunction, delivered within the hearing of all, that I should rehearse under my powers.

We proceed to the stage, where Mr Hough arranges with Mr Farron to position the company to my best advantage, both in the familiar arc at the floats and within the scenes. As usual, we begin with the business before turning to the dialogue where, fighting the urge to face my interlocutors, I recall Mr Hough's precept that I am the servant of the audience, at least those of rank and fashion in the boxes and of intellect and spirit in the pit.

'In London, it is considered a grave discourtesy to those who have commanded the spectacle and in whose name the action is undertaken, if the players converse among themselves as though nobody else were present,' he told me over breakfast. 'The key is to divide your attention, addressing your speeches to the house and turning back to the stage at their conclusion.'

Having rehearsed in an undertone, I am afraid that my voice might not carry in a theatre that is larger even than Glasgow. Mr Hough brushes aside my concern but, after the actors disperse, he makes me speak my lines with full force, while he paces up and down to ensure that I can be heard in every corner of the house. After a half-hour in which I recite speeches of Frederick and Romeo as well as Selim, he declares himself satisfied. My voice reaches the back of the upper gallery. There will be no catcalls.

After a second partial and a single group rehearsal, I am set to make my London debut. My first awareness of the weight of expectation comes, not from the cheers when I leave the hotel (which I innocently presume to be bestowed upon all debutants), but from the detachment of guards summoned to control the multitude, who have been gathering at the theatre since noon. Advised by the captain not to venture into the piazza, the coachman diverts our carriage down Long Acre and Hart Street.

Closeted in my dressing room, I escape the turmoil elsewhere in the building, but reports reach me from all sides. The press at the doors is so great that they are opened before time, prompting a stampede through the vestibule. Within minutes, all the passageways and corridors are blocked, with patrons caught in the crush fearing for their lives. Several people faint, and the removal of their insensate bodies leads to a spate of rumours that they have been trampled to death. Even this does not deter the crowds outside, who break windows and ram the newly locked doors in their determination to gain admittance, or the crowds inside, who tear down the balustrades in their determination to obtain seats. Gentlemen, unable to enter the pit for which they hold checks, assail the boxes: some risking the drop to the lower floor; others refusing to make way for the legitimate occupants when they arrive. One pugnacious pair turn their pistols on each other, and only the swift action of the peace officers prevents their exchanging fire. Little gallantry is shown to the ladies, whose views of the stage are obscured. Persons of the highest rank, who sent their footmen to secure their places earlier in the day, are unable to breach the throng, leaving the servants to enjoy the performance of which they have been deprived.

The heat in the house is so intense that the audience, which includes the Prince of Wales, Mr Pitt, Mr Fox and many of the dukes, duchesses, lords and ladies, who are to become my most fervent admirers and, if I may say so, friends, sit in extreme discomfort. No doubt this accounts for the uncivil reception of Mr Charles Kemble, when he enters to deliver an address especially penned for the occasion and which, in turn, accounts for his subsequent coldness towards me.

The shouts of 'Off! Off! Off!' that greet him are audible even in the dressing room, where I await my entrance, garbed in Selim's white linen pantaloons, short russet fur-trimmed jacket and white-and-gold turban. Mr Hough always pays the strictest attention to my costumes, puffing up the ruffles in my sleeves, smoothing out the creases in my shirt and trunks . . . no! Whatever Wilson might insinuate, he merely wants me to be seen to my best advantage. Where was I? Oh yes, waiting for Selim's entrance. For once its deferral to the second act is superfluous; there is no need to build up anticipation, which is so heightened that, when Mrs Litchfield and Mrs Henry Siddons come off stage, they protest that they might as well have been playing in a dumb show. Finally, the call boy summons me. Maybe it is the blithe assurance of youth, but I feel no apprehension. I am doing what I love for people who love what I do, and I adjudge myself the most fortunate boy in the land.

'"The secret pledge
Restor'd, prevents suspicion of the deed,
While it confirms it done.'"

Mr Hargrave gives me my cue and I walk on to the platform, to be greeted by absolute silence, rent by a jibe from the gallery of 'Here comes Aladdin. Where is your lamp?' The joker is roundly hissed, and I make my bow to thunderous applause, which is repeated regularly at the end – and twice in the middle – of my speeches during my first scene with Othman.

That scene alone offers me scope for so many fine points: the joyful declaration of 'Selim is yet alive'; the measured lifting of my turban to disclose the scar that proves my identity; the scornful recital of my dispatch of the slave whom Barbarossa has sent to slay me; the tentative, tender-voiced enquiry as to my mother's suffering, followed by the rapid gaze to heaven that will reward her virtues; the abrupt drawing of the dagger that will seal the tyrant's fate, which I clasp to my breast as if to anoint it with my blood; the martial determination to effect my revenge, followed by the filial devotion with which I appeal to my father's shade to assist me.

Then, as I lead Othman off stage, 'unaw'd by peril, pain or death,' I employ one of Mr Hough's studied pauses. By turning my back to the house, I give the impression of being struck by a secret thought or a sudden recollection. It always delights the audience and affords them the opportunity to speculate on my purpose – or, as Mr Hough puts it, to contemplate my person.

With similar points throughout the play, it is no surprise that Selim is one of my most cherished characters and
has long been favoured by audiences: so much so that on
several occasions they have refused to allow an afterpiece to
be given, lest it sully the emotion that my performance has
evoked. Even those who enter the theatre after the third
act are sufficiently moved by what they see not to object
to the truncation of the evening's entertainment. Which is
why, although I originally thought to make my return as
Essex or Alexander or Lothair, moustachioed and bearded
withal, I have acceded to the management's request to do
so as Selim, trusting that many a memory will be revived as
happily as my own.

The first two musics have gently underscored my reminiscences but, when the orchestra strikes up the third, a jaunty
medley of military airs that accords more with the wider
scene of war than with Mrs Centlivre's comedy, I turn my
attention to the stage. My neighbours are less courteous.
With neither Mrs Jordan nor Mr Charles Kemble, her
Felix, appearing until the second act, they chatter so loudly
among themselves that we might be observing Don Lopez's
plot and his daughter Isabella's plight through a pane of
glass.

When Mrs Jordan finally makes her bow, I am shocked
by the listless applause. It is true that the last six years have
added more to her girth than to her fame – her face, always
round, is now more chin than cheek – but surely the public
retains its affection for the favourite, who has entertained
them royally for so long? Or perhaps that *royally* is the
source of their disaffection? Even in faraway Shropshire
they spoke of how, after twenty years at his side and having

borne him ten children, she had received her congé from the Duke. Some pitied her, but most regarded it as just requital for a dissolute life.

They, who had never seen her schoolboy scrapes as Little Pickle or heard her voice like an exultation of larks as Rosalind and Mrs Cheerly, at least had some excuse. But what of the London audience, who had taken her to their hearts? Having once laughed with her, they now laugh at her. That look with which she greets her alleged resemblance to a nun may be a touch more wistful, but it remains as beguiling as ever; nevertheless it is met with derision. Likewise, although Violante is innocent, they prefer to endorse Felix's suspicions of her guilt, cheering every reference to her treason and abandonment to vice. Mr Charles Kemble beams so broadly at the approbation for his 'What hast thou to do with honour, thou that canst admit plurality of lovers?' that he must assume it is in response to his playing. Meanwhile, Mrs Jordan's dignity and poise confirm that it is her critics and not herself who are unworthy. From her spirit and sparkle, one would think her deaf to any sound that does not issue from the stage.

When the curtain falls, my desire to renew such a treasured acquaintance overcomes my reluctance to intrude on her grief. Fearing to lose myself in the unfamiliar passageways, I quit the theatre and make my way to the stage door. I give my name to the keeper, who shows no sign of recognition, and watch the actors, musicians and supernumeraries hurry away, as if they had been toiling in one of the factories of the north. I slip into the shadows when Mr Charles Kemble walks past with Mr Moody, their rivalry discarded with their costumes, since I have no wish to anticipate my meeting with his brother tomorrow. Finally, a woman approaches, who, while looking twenty years older without the wig and face powder, is instantly discernible as Violante. I can scarcely contain my relief when she introduces herself as Miss Hester Bland, and, with a jangling laugh that sounds like a parody of her younger sister, leads me to Mrs Jordan's room.

I find her at her table, lit by a single candle, gazing into the glass as if waiting, not for the door to open, but the flat-scenes to slide apart and discover her to the audience.

'Master Betty,' she says, rising and bobbing a curtsey.

'Mister Betty,' I say firmly, although I am aware that any allusion to the passage of time must be painful to her.

'Of course, of course. You can no longer enjoy the freedom of the actresses' dressing rooms.' I start, having no recollection of any rooms other than my own. 'You must forgive me. Had I thought, I would never have received you in dishabille.' Her hands flutter about her bosom, drawing attention to the very flesh that she professes a wish to conceal. She directs me to a chair beside an ornate writing desk, which she explains had been in her room at Drury Lane during the fire. 'Two carpenters risked immolation to rescue it. Imagine! Of course I rewarded them handsomely.'

'Improvidently,' Miss Bland interjects.

'All the rest was enflamed. Twenty years of costumes burnt to ashes.'

'Thirty.'

'Twenty years of costumes burnt to ashes!' Mrs Jordan repeats, as if silencing a hiss. 'Peggy, Rosalind, Lady Teazle, Miss Prue: nothing but memories.'

'But such glorious memories. No one will ever forget Mrs Jordan.'

She turns to me with a look of tearful gratitude, which Miss Bland cuts short. 'It is late, Dora. The supper will be on the table.'

'Then you must go ahead, Hester dear.' Mrs Jordan's steely expression belies her genial tone. 'No matter that I am the one who has laboured all evening, I would not wish to deny you your meal. Take the carriage and leave me to talk to Master Betty.'

'Mister—'

'But Dora, I cannot leave you in your dressing room, alone with a man.'

'It is not "a man"; it is Master Betty.'

'Mr Betty,' I say, with a squeak that almost justifies her resolve to eunuchize me.

'Yes of course, my dear. I mean no offence. But you and I are old friends, are we not? Go home, Hester, I said. Why are you waiting?'

Without a word of farewell, Miss Bland turns on her heel and sweeps out. Mrs Jordan looks as relieved as if she had removed her stays. 'Poor Hester, so intent on preserving my character. She refuses to accept that I am lost cargo.'

Tongue-tied, I fear that in the gloom my commiserative smile is of little comfort. She draws her peignoir closely around herself.

'It gives me great pleasure to see you again. I had thought that . . . no matter. Let us recall happier days, when you had the whole town at your feet.'

'Happy, yes, but with one lasting regret.'

'What was that?'

'That I never acted with Mrs Jordan.'

'Really?' She sounds surprised. 'Oh no, that would never have done. It was most gratifying to see the Brother and the

Sister brought down a peg. But as to acting with you, that was out of the question.'

It is my turn to be surprised. She must mean that the town would never have countenanced a woman of her notoriety acting alongside a boy. I determine to reassure her, but she forestalls me. 'I was saddened to hear that you were once again treading the boards. Do you want for funds? You were recompensed more richly than any of us. Or did that wretched father of yours squander it all?'

'Not at all. He invested it wisely. I have an estate in Shropshire.' Determined to defend Papa even beyond the grave, I say nothing of my great-uncle's legacy.

'Then why subject yourself to the torment . . . the back-biting . . . the ingratitude? Or do you still profess that it is for love?'

I hang my head, as if the admission were shameful.

'Oh my dear boy, there were those who claimed that your modesty was your finest performance, but I always said that you were sincere.'

'How can you not love the stage on which you have known such triumphs?'

'If I were bald, would you ask me if I loved my wig? I have no other recourse. I have to provide for my children.'

'Does not the Duke . . . ? I beg pardon, it is not my place.'

'I have three older daughters, not to mention their husbands. They look to me to discharge their liabilities, just as certain exalted personages look to the Privy Purse. The Siddons was more fortunate. She retired last summer with a performance of the Scottish queen and now commits herself to nothing more exacting than the occasional recital. And as for assisting her children! When her son Henry secured the Edinburgh patent and was in desperate need of a sure attraction, his mother refused to appear except for her usual terms of half the receipts and a clear benefit. Yet she is deemed to have brought a new propriety to the profession. She is received at Kew and at Buckingham House where, at the Queen's command, she reads to the princesses – those same princesses who have never acknowledged me with a single word, even though I lived with their brother for twenty years and gave them ten nephews and nieces.'

I feel deep sympathy for a woman who has been cruelly maligned. I recall someone – I suspect that it was Mr Northcote when I sat for my portrait – explaining that it was she who replenished the royal coffers and not the other way round. The destitute duke had insisted that she continue to grace the stage with her elegance and charm, long after the stage had ceased to enchant her. Moreover, far from setting out to entrap him, she had resisted his advances until the widespread assumption that she had succumbed to them rendered further resistance futile.

'For all those years there were persons close to the throne who seized every chance to slander me. They insinuated that, when I went on tour, my chamber door was permanently ajar. Of course, the Duke scorned to give their calumnies credence. But how different is the treatment of male and female, even when the one is guilty and the other blameless! I was present on the night that Mr Kemble attempted to ravish Maria de Camp after the performance of *The Plain Dealer*. He had played Manly, I Fidelia and she Eliza. I heard her cries for help and ran to her dressing room. Her dress was torn; his breeches undone. Forgive me if this is unsuitable—'

'I am twenty-one years old.'

'True. The fault is yours for making such an indelible

impression as a boy. He was drunk and debauched and she half-dead with fright. Yet all he had to do was post an apology in the newspapers, and his wife, his friends and even the public forgave him. I was faithful to a man for twenty years. I was his wife in all but name . . . that name which was the one thing he could never give me. Then when he cast me aside to woo an heiress, as brazenly as Petruchio in the play, my critics – worse, my former admirers – showed me no mercy. I appealed to his brother, but he, who had oft-times assured me of his undying esteem, failed so much as to reply to my letter. There again, why should he heed a mere actress – no longer his brother's devoted helpmeet but his discarded doxy?'

The epithet jars and I fear that she is working herself up into a tirade worthy of Mrs Siddons. 'I know what it is to fall from favour,' I say. 'We are cut from the same cloth.'

'No!' she cries, as if my words had stung her. 'Not at all. The public still favours me. Of course they laugh when I speak a line that seems to betoken my history, but they laugh with me. I am their own "sweet Nell", although her fate was kinder than mine; her royal lover never deserted her. "Let not poor Nelly starve!" Huh! *The Times* reviles my every appearance, as if my place in the theatre were akin to that of the harlots who haunt the saloons and the basket boxes. They maintain that audiences only come to see me out of salacity, but I have no need to explain that to you.'

I give her a guarded smile and wish that I were more conversant with *salacity*.

'Yet if I were so minded, I could be as scarlet as they paint. On my last visit to Dublin in 1809' – she stares at the glass as if to convince herself that little has changed since then – 'I received the gallantries (ill-judged and instantly rebuffed) of the Lord Lieutenant himself. Even though he sat only a few feet away from me in the stage box, he still saw the young woman from twenty or so years before.' She trembles with indignation, which I suspect is not unmixed with pride. 'I was playing Peggy in *The Country Girl*.'

'I beg to differ.'

'I think I may be trusted to know my own role.'

'Playing truant from my studies at Cambridge, I delved into theatrical chronicles. To a man, the writers declare that you did not play Peggy. You *were* Peggy.'

'Why thank you, young sir. You have learned to praise most prettily.'

'I myself saw the play but once, without the genius of Mrs Jordan, and found it altogether lacking in charm. It contented the house no more than it did me. I have no recollection even of where it took place.'

'No recollection whatsoever?' Her expression is harder to decipher than any she exhibited as Violante.

'None.'

'Then it is not for me to remedy the lapse. Now you must leave me. My sister will not be alone in rueing my tardiness. I am to play Widow Cheerly tomorrow night.'

'And I shall be cheering you as loudly as ever.'

'Thank you.' She moves towards me and takes my hand, her touch as soft as a purr. 'And thank you for coming. You bring back so many souvenirs. Happy days!'

'They were indeed. Was there one role in particular that pleased you?' I wait for the obligatory Norval.

'Not on the stage, you noodle! At Bushy. I see you now romping around the park with George and Henry. Coursing hares with Roger – no, Robin – the farmer. Climbing the great oak while that tutor of yours stood trembling at the base, terrified lest you should fall. Surely you remember?'

'Yes, of course. How could I forget?'

The week that I spent with the Duke and Mrs Jordan at Bushy Park is one of the abiding memories of my boyhood. I had fallen ill. My exertions on the stage, followed by my nightly attendance at suppers and receptions, had taken their toll. I was confined to bed. Ladies of quality sent sweetmeats and possets and claret jelly, the very fare that, according to Mama, had caused me to sicken. So many well-wishers left cards that straw was laid on the cobbles in front of our lodgings to deaden the noise of their carriages. Nothing, however, could muffle the anxiety of the assembled crowd; the physicians were obliged to post bulletins on the gate to relieve it. Papa reported that the town spoke of little but the king's state of mind and my state of health. My performances were cancelled and even the box owners curbed their annoyance, for fear that I should never return. I was prescribed a regimen of hot baths and cream of tartar, and my constitution, hardy enough for the swordplay at the end of *Gustavus Vasa* and *Hamlet*, was rapidly restored.

As soon as I was pronounced fit to travel, the Duke and Mrs Jordan invited me to Bushy to take the country air. Mama was loath to accept, although I cannot recall (if, indeed, I ever knew) whether she wished me to eschew society in general or simply that of Mrs Jordan. But Papa slapped her down – no, not *slapped*, that is the wrong word, quite the wrong word; *shouted*, that is better. He shouted her down, and off we went.

Since my first meeting with Prince William Frederick in Liverpool, I had been smiled upon by royalty. In London, the Prince of Wales and his brothers regularly attended my performances. But it was the Duke of Clarence who was my greatest champion. He was a bluff and jovial man, with a face that looked to have been scoured of all passion like a pebble on a beach. Whether his attachment to Mrs Jordan had sharpened his sympathy for her fellow players or his dispatch to sea at fourteen had sparked his appreciation of youthful endeavour I cannot say, but he lost no opportunity to serve me. He asked me to dine in Parliament and, to the dismay of his equerries, exhorted me to sit on the throne. He accompanied me to sittings in Mr Northcote's studio, seeking to divert me by pulling faces behind his back and cracking jests about his diminutive size and irregular dress until, displaying scant respect for rank, the painter showed him the door.

He took it in good part and Mr Northcote was among the company a few days later, when we visited the Tower and the Duke commanded the Lieutenant to fire a cannon in my honour. We climbed up to the battlements which, to my delight, were exactly as the scene painters had rendered them for the opening of *Richard III*, and down to the White Tower, where the Duke pointed out the spot beneath the chapel staircase where the bones of the two murdered princes had been unearthed. I failed to suppress a shudder, prompting Papa to hiss that King Richard was one of the Duke's ancestors and Mr Hough to mutter that such squeamishness would impair my performance of the Crookback.

We visited the Armoury and the Jewel House and, most exciting of all, the Menagerie, where the Duke, whose kindness was not untinged with cruelty, informed me that the entrance fee was nine pence or a cat or dog to be fed to the lions. There were indeed two lion cubs roaming the compound and I was allowed to pet them, along with wolves, a hyena, a grizzly bear, a kangaroo and a zebra, which I rode for a few paces, until Mr Hough, fearing that I would slip off and scrape my face, made me dismount. Finally, we visited the Monkey Room, only to beat a hasty retreat when the motions of a shameless baboon were a vexation to the gentlemen, an abhorrence to the ladies, and an acute embarrassment to a thirteen-year-old boy.

'You have fallen silent,' Mrs Jordan says.

'Forgive me. I was thinking of George and Henry,' I reply, reluctant to admit that I had been thinking of their father. 'They welcomed me so warmly.'

'They rebelled when I told them you were coming. They thought that you would be puffed up.'

'But they were the grandsons of the king!'

'Who has yet to acknowledge them . . . They soon discovered their mistake. I know that we are none of us the same persons before the lamps as we are outside of the theatre, but it was unnerving to see you flying kites, collecting eggs and taming pigeons, after hearing your Osmond spit curses at Percy or Frederick thunder reproaches at Baron Wildenhaim.'

Of course! The line that repeatedly sneaks into my brain is Frederick's in *Lover's Vows*.

Why should I ever know my father, if he is a villain? My heart is satisfied with a mother.

Thankful to have discovered its source, I resolve to banish it.

'I fear that George and I were not always kind to young Henry.'

'It can have done him no harm. He is now with his regiment in the Peninsular. As is George.'

'You must be very proud.'

'I am.' She averts her head, but I hear the joy in her voice. 'And fearful. Very fearful.'

'Do they write?'

'To their father. I receive news through their sisters. They have so little time; one letter must suffice for all.' She breathes heavily. 'Now I really must send you away or we will be here until breakfast.'

'Forgive me, I have detained you.'

'No, you have delighted me. Master . . . Mister Betty, will you do an old woman a kindness and be Master Betty one last time, permitting me to give you a mother's kiss?'

'I would be honoured.'

She approaches and, laying both hands on my cheeks, plants a kiss on my brow. To my surprise, her lips are dry. I stay still for a moment. Then with a low bow, I quit the room before my tears unman me.

5

The blast of a horn tears through my dream. For an instant, the unfamiliar chamber confuses me and I suspect that I am still asleep. Then a cry of 'Bloody news! Bloody news!', followed by a second blast, restores me to my senses. Throwing a gown over my nightshirt, I summon Mrs Stirling, hand her the sixpence halfpenny, and dispatch her into the piazza to purchase the *Morning Chronicle*. As soon as she returns, I open the paper to discover that the sanguinary event in question is the hanging of sixteen frame-breakers in York. I pity the poor wretches who, had they been better schooled, would have learnt the lesson of King Canute. Nonetheless, I am grateful that it was their necks that were broken and not those of the soldiers battling Buonaparte's tyranny in Spain.

The faces of George and Henry Fitzclarence appear before me, and I reflect on my last night's visit to the theatre. Did my conference with their mother provoke my present excess of melancholy, or was it rather the remembrance of my own endeavours on the stage? Although their strictures were carefully concealed from me, I am aware that critics judged my roles to be unsuited to my years. As Rolla and Vasa, I played officers when twelve months before I had been marshalling my tin soldiers. As Richard and Osmond, I played seducers when my loins were no more aflame than my fingers. As Hamlet, I pondered the ways of providence when I still knelt prayerfully by my bedside at night. Yet if the audience remarked on the disparity, they paid it no heed. So was everyone, from the royal box to the shilling gallery, consumed by madness? Or were they making mock of me, like the boys in Ballynahinch who pinned the dead cat to the simpleton's coat-tails? All in all, is it not more likely that the statesmen and generals, the lawyers and wits, the lords and ladies, the bankers and merchants and, yes, the butchers, the bakers, the candlestick makers and their wives, were sincere in their praise of my playing?

I silence any lingering doubts, as I button my shirt and leave to breakfast at New Slaughter's coffee house in St Martin's Lane. Replenished, I make my way to the theatre, a full two hours before the rehearsal is set to start. I give my name to the stage doorkeeper who, from his dishevelment, looks to have slept in his booth. He shows no more sign of recognising me than he did last night; indeed, he shows no sign of recognising me from last night. He summons the under-prompter to apprise Mr Kemble of my arrival. My pounding heart is only slightly stilled when he qualifies the name with a *Charles*.

Stepping out on to the stage, I view the house, which is as sombre by day as it was brilliant at night. My childhood fascination with the world behind the scenes has never waned, and I thrill to the bustle, watching as a carpenter or scene-shifter accosts a laundress or seamstress (his box of tools and her bundle of dresses afford no further clues). His smile fades as she pokes him so hard in the chest that he narrowly avoids a tumble. Looking both angry and per-plexed, he curses an errand boy who, ignorant of theatrical custom, saunters across the stage, whistling.

The under-prompter, announcing himself as Ambrose

Crowther, escorts me to the manager's office, where Charles Kemble in his shirt-sleeves, sits reading. Hastily donning his coat, he welcomes me to the theatre, 'newly built, but no conflagration can erase Master Betty's fame.' I thank him and, after expressing my pleasure at returning, felicitate him on his Felix. 'You are most kind. As you may imagine, the estimate of so practised a player as yourself signifies a great deal.' He speaks with such earnestness that I resolve to take him at his word, even though I have Mr Hough's voice in my head, chiding my credulity. 'I was surprised to learn that you were rejoining our ranks. But then there were those who said that all you lacked was an education to render you the first player in the annals of the stage. No doubt you wish to validate their faith.'

'I wish to make myself as useful a player as I can,' I say, unease prompting me to accept a glass of madeira from Mr Crowther, even though the clock has just chimed ten. 'I was most grateful to receive Mr Kemble's offer of engagement. I presume that he has heard reports of my reception across the country?'

'He has seen copies of the receipts. Expedience ever supersedes discernment.'

'I had hoped that he would be here to greet me.'

'He and Mrs Kemble are making a short expedition through Ireland. The management of the theatre grows ever more onerous. My sister made her farewell in June yet, even beforehand, the most popular nights were not hers and my brother's but Mr Grimaldi's in the pantomime.'

'Grimaldi? He acted with me in *Hamlet*. He assisted Mr Suett as the gravedigger. He had but a handful of lines.'

'He dislikes lines,' Charles Kemble replies mordantly.

'But I shall never forget his face when Mr Suett peeled

off his waistcoats – all eight of them – one by one. The audience howled with laughter. It made my speech to the skull all the more poignant.'

'It was heart-rending,' Mr Crowther interjects, 'to see such a sensitive, silver-tongued boy confronting his mortality.'

'Yes, thank you,' Charles Kemble says sharply. 'Mr Grimaldi is here now, in *Harlequin and the Red Dwarf.* Tripping up an old crone, assaulting Pantaloon, playing tunes on a fish kettle and leapfrog with a man-size frog. As you can appreciate, it is the apogee of the dramatic art.'

'I should like to see it.'

'But then, catering to the taste of the town, my brother was obliged last year to hire sixteen of Mr Astley's white horses. They pranced around the stage; they neighed prettily. And now he offers them the return of Master Betty. Need I say more?'

'No,' I reply. 'He offers them the debut of Mr Betty.'

'Oh my dear sir,' Charles Kemble says, looking at me with unexpected warmth. 'If you believe that, then heaven help you!'

Mr Crowther leads me to my dressing room, which, although adjacent to the stage, offers a less direct view than I enjoyed in the old building. He clacks inconsequentially and I interject at intervals, loath to betray my hurt at Charles Kemble's imputation. I do not prance or neigh; I am a player not a pleasure-ground attraction! By every measure, he is the lesser Kemble. I am dismayed to find that he still blames me for the slight he received eight years ago at my first performance. What other reason can he have for such a grudging welcome? Unlike his brother and sister, laid low with severe ailments, he acted alongside me several times. I search my memory for any occasion when, wearied as much by the hubbub in the house as by my exertions on the stage, I might have shown him a casual discourtesy, and I find none. Instead, I see him whispering in corners, as though the intrigues of the play had been extended to the green room, and I feel the ferocity of his thrusts as Laertes and Richmond, as though he were fighting not just in his character's right but his own.

Dismissing Mr Crowther's offer to rehearse my dialogue, I take out the length, dog's-eared and faded, that has accompanied me since I first played Selim in Belfast. The speeches and cues in Mr Hough's spidery hand are as much a talisman as an aide-memoire. Selim's courage, as he returns to claim his throne, shames my apprehension as I return to claim mine. I remind myself that I am here at the invitation of Mr Kemble. Unlike his brother, he has good reason to resent me, so his readiness to engage me must betoken his esteem.

I blush to recall how I was the unwitting agent of his humiliation. Although I honoured – indeed, idolised – him, there were many, even among the cognoscenti, who held that he laboured his effects, lacking the spark and spontaneity that Garrick and – here, my blush deepens – I brought to our impersonations. They presented the contrast between us as that between Nature and Art, whereas I regard it rather as that between Youth and Age. From the start, critics were intent on setting us at odds. Treating the stage like a boxing booth, they willed me to bloody his nose.

Having declined to attend the rehearsals for my earlier performances, Mr Kemble came to assist me as Hamlet, a part in which he had triumphed and to which he was especially attached. He declared that he owed it to the company and, indeed, it was he who had assigned them their roles. I mean no disrespect to my fellow players, when I say that I recall very few of them. Mrs Litchfield, who played my mother, not just in *Hamlet* but in *Barbarossa* and *Zara*, was jovial and stout, with wisps of white hair peeping through her brown daytime wig. Mrs Taylor, who played Ophelia, smelt of sweet peas and fed me marchpane mice, which I nibbled to spare her feelings even though they made me bilious. Mr Munden, who played Polonius, pulled faces to divert me in the side-wings and to distract me when he was dead. Mr Murray, who played the Ghost, refused to enter a scene in which anyone was wearing blue. But I acted with so many Horatios, Marcelluses and Osrics, both in town and across the country, that I am no longer able to distinguish them.

The Claudius was Mr Cooke, whose recent death I lament even though he terrified me, and not just when we clashed on the stage. He had a voice like a blade being whetted on a stone and the most beaklike nose I have ever seen. His 'over-fondness for the grape' – an expression that delighted my auditors when, in my innocence, I confessed that I shared it – lent him a daunting unpredictability. I have read that Macklin bathed every night in brandy, a practice to which he ascribed his longevity; Cooke soaked himself in a more conventional way, which no doubt contributed to his early demise.

One night, which is forever stamped on my mind, he arrived a mere five minutes before the first music, protesting that he had been drilling with the Volunteers at Chalk Farm. He flung a cloak over his muddy militia coat and staggered towards the stage, where he hiccupped unintelligible sounds before seizing Mrs Lichfield's hand and leading her through the proscenium door. As Hamlet, I was the last to enter and the burst of applause, which I fear he misconstrued, appeared to rouse him. He weathered the first scene, after which a good half of his part was played out in the prompt corner. Mr Hough, ever ready to accuse Mr Kemble of perfidy, alleged that he had cast him in order to sabotage my performance. Mr Cooke, meanwhile, sought to hit back at his long-time rival. Squeezing my shoulder and suffocating me with his foetid breath, he croaked: 'You and me, my lad, together we'll cut Black Jack Kemble's comb!'

I was but a boy – it bears repeating: but a boy.

I cannot recollect Mr Cooke's ever attending a rehearsal. No doubt he considered the five-shilling fine a lesser imposition. Likewise, Mr Kemble and Mr Farron must have felt it futile to remonstrate with one who would follow his own inclination, regardless of their reproof. In any event, the *Hamlet* rehearsal that has lodged in my memory is not with the king but with the ghost.

Mr Kemble, Mr Hough and Mr Farron, together with the under-prompter (not yet Mr Crowther) and copyists, are seated at the edge of the platform. I enter with Horatio and Marcellus from the right-hand proscenium door . . . No, I am mistaken, Mr Kemble is yet to arrive. He does so while Mr Hough is insisting that my fellow players stand further downstage of me during my speech about the shameful inebriation of my countrymen (a speech, I might add, that Mr Cooke would have done well to heed).

'A thousand pardons. I was unavoidably detained. Pray

ignore me,' Mr Kemble says, although he must know that that is as impossible as if a lion prowled the stage. 'I shall sit quietly here.' The very chair creaks as though in rebuttal. 'I am come to do all in my meagre power to assist Master Betty's impersonation.'

He has graced several of my performances in despite of the very audible affliction of his lungs, yet I feel more nervous – more vulnerable – now that I face him alone, without the support of my audience. He nods approvingly when I take up my attitude, only to exclaim in surprise (which, in retrospect, appears contrived) when Mr Hough explains that I am to walk towards the back of the scenes, while my two companions remain on the platform and the ghost rises from the trap.

'Look, my lord, it comes!' Horatio says. I turn of a sudden and reel back, following Mr Hough's instruction to envisage 'a football . . . no, better still, a snowball with a stone within it hitting you in the chest.' I bend at the knee, raising both arms to my head (but not an inch higher), stretching my fingers and opening my mouth in a precise attitude of terror. I commence my speech: 'Angels and ministers of grace defend us.' Addressing the ghost as 'Hamlet, king, father, royal Dane,' I lean forward and clutch my brow, while remembering Mr Hough's precept that sorrow is an emotion best expressed with the eyes and face rather than the hands. Mr Kemble coughs but, uncertain whether it is the same complaint that has punctuated several of my soliloquies or a studied interruption, I carry on until he speaks.

'If I may offer a humble suggestion that in no way detracts from the splendour of Master Betty's playing.'

'Pray do,' Mr Hough says.

'The prince's initial response on seeing the ghost is indeed one of consternation, but he swiftly takes command of his passions. As the volley of questions indicates, his principal concern is for information. Why . . . wherefore . . . what? It is surely an error for him to wallow – however prettily – in grief.'

'That is a most interesting reading, but I regret fallacious,' Mr Hough replies, as equably as a magistrate passing a sentence of death before dinner. 'An intellectual appraisal that no doubt brings comfort to actors too old for the primal, filial passions that the Young Roscius conveys.'

A silence descends, which reveals the depth of his rancour even to one who struggles to follow his argument. On reflection, I wonder whether Wilson was right, at least in that respect, and Mr Kemble's brutal verdict on his performance in York poisoned his life.

'Had you had the good fortune to see the Young Roscius' Hamlet in Edinburgh or Sheffield or Birmingham – and I assure you that, notwithstanding the crush, we would have secured you a seat – you would have witnessed a performance of a truth and naturalness that has not been seen on the British stage since the death of Garrick.'

'Garrick had a cord fitted to his wig, which he pulled so that his hair rose on end at the advent of the ghost. Is that truthful? Is that natural?'

'There was more truth in Garrick's wig than in some actors' entire bodies.'

'This is insufferable!'

'Gentlemen, please!' Mr Farron interposes. 'We have much to do. I suggest that we continue from "It waves me still. Go on, I'll follow thee".'

Disoriented, I walk towards the left-hand proscenium

door and am relieved that the movement draws no comment. Horatio and Marcellus seek to detain me, whereupon I draw my sword and point it at Horatio's neck.

'Is he going to do it like that?' asks Mr . . . it is no use. Try as I might, I cannot recall his name. 'Mr Kemble merely lifts the hilt of his sword from its sheath.'

'The threat is enough to deter them,' Mr Kemble says.

'Indeed it would be,' Mr Hough replies, 'had they been disputing in mid-afternoon in the castle forecourt. But they are walking the battlements at midnight. Hamlet – the Young Roscius – is distracted. He does not know where the ghost will lead him. So, yes, he presses the naked blade to Horatio's throat. Carry on, William!'

I exit through the right-hand door and cross in front of the scenes, which will, I trust, depict turrets and parapets rather than the current sylvan setting, the effect enhanced by the wind machine and orchestra. As I follow Mr Murray back on through the left-hand door, Mr Kemble remarks in a penetrating whisper: 'I see that he is still pointing his sword. This time at the ghost. Does he not know that he is insubstantial and unable to do him harm? Surely it makes more sense to let it trail behind?' I stop and look at him. 'Oh, a thousand pardons. I was musing to myself. Pay me no heed.'

'So should I drag the sword, as if I have forgotten that I am holding it?' I pluck up the courage to address him for the first time.

'It has proved powerful in the past, although I say so myself.'

'Shall I try it?' I ask Mr Hough.

'No,' he replies emphatically. 'You are yet to discover whether he is a spirit of health or a goblin damned. You must be on your guard.'

'Keeping him at bay and yet stricken with grief for him,' Mr Kemble says. 'Is that not inconsistent?'

'We all admire the way that you settle on the ruling passion of a character and never deviate from it in the slightest regard. But the Young Roscius finds the appropriate passion for each scene, each speech, each line, to the glory of the play and the relish of the audience. Carry on, William!'

Horrified that Mr Hough should have upbraided Mr Kemble in company, I fear that the sole passion I can summon is embarrassment. My one consolation is that we are rehearsing the business and not the lines. Mr Murray, clearly as keen to escape as I am, trims his long expository speech to 'adulterous beast . . . virtuous queen . . . celestial bed . . . loathsome crust . . . smooth body . . . O, horrible! O, horrible! Most horrible! . . . Remember me.' To a smattering of laughter and applause, he squats to mime descending in the trap before marching off the stage. I rush through the speech prior to Horatio and Marcellus' entrance, fearing that Mr Hough will seize on 'And you, my sinews, grow not instant old, but bear me stiffly up' to launch a further broadside against Mr Kemble, since he has previously declared this stiffness to be the keynote of his impersonation. Much to my relief, he says nothing, until Horatio and Marcellus' arrival creates fresh friction.

'How is't, my noble lord?' Marcellus says.

'Are you not going to say "Illo, ho, ho, my lord!"?' I ask.

'Mr Kemble – we – cut all the "wild and whirling words",' Horatio says.

'They are beneath the prince's dignity,' Mr Kemble adds.

'Some players need to stand on their dignity. The Young Roscius' dignity is innate,' Mr Hough says, before turning to Mr Farron. 'I explained that the lines were to be rein-stated. Have the actors not received the new lengths?'

'I issued instructions,' Mr Farron says, glowering at the copyist, who seeks to exculpate himself.

Struggling to contain his hacking cough and trembling hands, Mr Kemble addresses Mr Hough. 'No doubt you intend to revive the absurdity of Hamlet calling his father "an old mole"?'

'Absurd to whom?' Mr Hough asks.

'To Hamlet, to the audience, to the author himself. Even as one who has made the play his peculiar study for more than thirty years, I would not presume to challenge Master Betty's dramatic tutor did I not have the voice of several eminent scholars that the phrase is a remnant of the source play, appropriated from a very different character.'

'An interesting hypothesis, to be sure. But you may be confident that the Young Rosicus will do justice to every aspect of the character as written.'

'In which case, I trust that you will retain Hamlet's advice to the players,' Mr Kemble says, as he staggers up, wheezing. 'Unless you fear that his instruction not to tear a passion to tatters might sound incongruous, indeed hypo-critical, on Master Betty's lips.'

'Not at all,' Mr Hough replies smoothly. 'The Young Roscius is a newcomer here and it would be discourteous of him, even in the person of Hamlet, to give advice to those who have "strutted and bellowed" for so long . . . so very long.'

'What about Rosencrantz's denunciation of the boy actors? Surely such a versatile and well-rounded Hamlet as Master Betty will be able to laugh off any awkwardness about the "aerie of children", the "little eyases", who are "most tyrannically clapped"?'

'Which children? What is an eyases?' I ask.

'Quiet, William!'

Mr Kemble approaches me. Rasping and spluttering and fixing me with a piercing stare, he declaims. '"What are they children? Who maintains 'em? How are they escoted? Will they pursue the quality no longer than they can sing? Will they not say afterwards if they should grow themselves to be common players (as it is like most will if their means are not better) their tutors do them wrong, to make them exclaim against their own succession?"'

'The word is *writers*,' Mr Hough says. 'You must have a corrupt text.'

'I used the word purposedly.'

Memory, like a rogue coachman, takes me to places that I have no desire to visit. Mr Kemble departs. I seem to see him stalking out, but that must be my fancy for he has a lameness in the right knee and, even on the stage, he limped. Mr Hough requests a short break, which Mr Farron grants, in despite of remonstrances from several of the players, who are eager to conclude their labours.

'That was very good work, William,' Mr Hough says, drawing me aside.

'I only did three scenes.'

'You did a great deal more than that. Did you not see the fury in Black Jack's eyes? If only he put half as much passion into his performances, he might have made a respectable player.'

'He is the first player in the land,' I say boldly.

'You are too modest! He should have stuck to his training. Did you know that he went to a Popish seminary in France? Which explains the singsong locution.'

'It is his asthma. He has an irritation on the lung.'

'I commiserate. But why must he burden the stage with it? There is one lesson you must learn in life, William – no, not you, since you have divine gifts denied to the rest of us – that is to know your limitations. Can a one-legged man be a soldier?'

I wish I had replied that a one-armed man could be a sailor, indeed the greatest sailor in the world, but my wits are honed in hindsight.

'We will leap from peak to peak, while Black Jack plods, leaden-footed, through the valley below.'

One under-prompter calls me back to the platform for the second act of *Hamlet*, even as another calls me to the platform for the second act of *Barbarossa*, and the first lines that I have uttered on a London stage, since I sank down beside the corpse of my dead love in *Tancred and Sigismunda* at Drury Lane six years ago. I am reunited with Mr Barrymore and Mrs Powell, themselves defectors from Drury Lane, as Othman and Zaphira, and introduced to Mr and Mrs Egerton as Barbarossa and Zara. All four greet me warmly and, after some desultory chit-chat, we begin the rehearsal, which, since my business is little different from that of Mr Young, the wonted possessor of the role, proceeds without impediment. I slip back into Selim as into a familiar suit of clothes, although, given that the breeches would have to be let out as well as down by several inches, the image is ill-chosen.

After we have discharged both the business and the dialogue, Mr Barrymore invites me to the Coal Hole, the tavern in Fountain Court frequented by actors from both houses, together with singers from the Sans Pareil and showmen from the Olympic. While eager to consolidate the amity (and to mark my arrival as an adult member of the profession), I politely decline, since I need more time to lay my ghosts.

Returning to the dressing room, I find them everywhere, lining the corridor and crowding the doorway, eager to salute me. They have been watching the performance, which I discern from the white ruffled collar and black doublet draped across the chair was *Hamlet*, and from the snatches of discourse my debut in the role.

The anticipation has been unparalleled. Patrons, desperate to secure their seats, are said to have suborned the watch-men to conceal them overnight about the theatre. Parliament passed a motion, proposed by Mr Pitt himself, that the House should rise early so that members might attend the play. The hunger to see me has outweighed the most pressing affairs of state, whether the building of the new docks or the raising of excise duties or even the conduct of the war. From the ovations I receive, I may say without risk of immodesty that the audience are not disappointed. They oblige me to repeat two soliloquies, and huzzahs and applause repeatedly interrupt my speeches. I am flustered only once, when I profess myself 'a rogue and peasant slave', and a gentleman in the pit jumps up with a shout of 'Never! A foul calumny!' Far from quieting him, his fellows clap and cry 'Hear! Hear!' Mr Hough, watching from the proscenium door, exhorts me to acknowledge the cheers with a reverence, which I do, only to lose my place twice in the subsequent lines. I am assured that the prompts are drowned out in the general clamour.

I deliver the remainder of my speeches without a single fault. The same cannot be said of Mr Cooke, who slurs so many of his lines in the prayer scene that the audience whistle and boo. Shaken, he walks down to the floats and craves their indulgence for his 'old complaint', which they might have been willing to grant had he not been grinning. The contempt for Claudius ensures that the approbation for Hamlet is all the greater and, when the curtain falls on my dying words, the applause is as ear-rending, if not more so, than that for my Norval in his native Scotland. Barely have I quit the stage than I collapse and am carried, insensate, to the dressing room. I am revived by Mr Hough holding a sponge, soaked in vinegar under my nose. My heart beats wildly and my chest rises and falls like a bellows. It slowly subsides, as he peels off my sopping shirt and rubs my chest and arms with the sponge, before pulling off my breeches and stockings, yet never touching my drawers, which, had Wilson's odious, unfounded aspersions contained one grain of truth, would surely have attracted his attention.

Papa arrives with four men. Mr Hough leaps up and hands me a shirt, which I throw over my head, although my skin is still damp.

'Mr Betty, please take these gentlemen out. The Young Roscius is in a state of undress.'

'Mr Hough, always so old-maidenish! William is quite proper. The Queen herself would have no call to avert her eyes.'

'On the contrary, she would feast them,' one of the men says, eliciting squeals of delight from his companions.

'I must protest—'

'Your protest is noted,' Papa says, the smile in his voice failing to dispel the glare in his eyes.

'Methinks the tutor doth protest too much!' says another man, occasioning further merriment. To my chagrin, I recognise him as the Bowbearer of the Forest of Bowland, but

I shall not speak of him. He may have tracked me across the country, but he has no more place in these memoirs than the women who sell oranges and playbills in the house – less, since they at least render a service.

'These gentlemen are your most ardent admirers, William,' Papa says. 'They have come to pay their respects.'

'I thank you, sir, for the most affecting night of my life,' one says.

'Have you forgotten your wedding night?' another asks him.

'I have not!' the first one says, with a grimace.

'I never dreamt I should see so perfect a performance. Men will speak of it as long as they have tongues.'

'Men will speak of it as long as there are men!'

'For the first time we have the Hamlet that Shakespeare intended,' the Bowbearer says, determined to make his presence felt, regardless of my resolve. 'The young prince eager to return to school but forced to abide in the venal world of adults, among tyrants, murderers, lickspittles, drunks and lechers. Yet through all that – and in despite of Ophelia's shameless overtures – his virtue remains unsullied. I can say no more; I am overwhelmed.'

He sinks into a chair, whereupon one of his companions grabs the sponge that Mr Hough set down and holds it to his brow. Another, seemingly sharing my embarrassment at his antics, turns to Papa. 'Among the many marvels of the performance, not the least was the duel. I gather that we have you to thank for that.'

'Indeed, I can claim a portion of the credit. I have instructed William in the noble art since infancy.'

'Papa is one of the first fencers in the land,' I say proudly.

'Was, William, was. I had my day.'

'Your salute before the bout began . . . the elegance of your advances . . . the delicacy of your parries, whereas Charles Kemble lunged at you as if he were warding off a band of caitiffs with his staff.'

'The error into which so many Hamlets fall is to antici-pate Laertes' treachery,' Mr Hough interjects. 'It is a courtly contest, not a fight to the death.'

'Thank you. I think that these gentlemen would have worked that out for themselves, without your pedagogical gloss.' Papa notices that I am sheltering behind the couch, shivering in my shirt and drawers, uncertain how to retrieve the rest of my clothes. 'Now, gentlemen, we must repair to the saloon while our young hero attires himself. We are expected at a fete at Lady Abercorn's. It would not do to disappoint her.'

'Oh no, Papa. I am worn out. Do I have to go?'

'Tut-tut, what is this? The fete is in your honour. The whole town wishes to commend your performance. Mr Pitt himself is among the guests.'

'May I not see him in the morning?'

'When do you suggest? When he is due to meet the military commanders, or the embassies from Russia and Austria, or perhaps the king? Now enough of this nonsense, or would you have him send me to the Tower?'

One of the visitors laughs, but I take the threat seriously. I cannot recall whether the Duke had taken me to the Tower by then or whether it loomed large in my imagination from my murder of King Henry and the Princes in *Richard III*. I never doubted that the prime minister, who could order admirals to set sail and generals into battle, could dispatch a mere country gentleman to prison, even putting him to the torture. I despair of my callowness now but, had I not been so impressible, I might never have become an actor.

'Of course not, Papa,' I reply, clinging to him.

'Very well, that's enough. Enough I say!' He thrusts me aside.

'Look at the teardrops in his eyes!' one of the men says.

'A paragon of filial affection!' his friend replies.

How I wish that I had rebelled! But I was as blind to my own interests as when, at the pinnacle of my fame, a circle of prominent gentlemen, alleging that Papa was enslaving me, appealed to the Lord Chancellor to order my removal from the stage until I attained the age of discretion. I was so fatigued by my nightly performances, followed by the receptions at which, like as not, I would be called upon to recite, that all the joy of acting had vanished, and I longed to return to the tranquillity of Ballynahinch. But when Lord Eldon summoned me in private and offered to put me under the protection of the Court of Chancery, I refused, after Papa persuaded me that, were I to accept, I would never see Mama or Marianne again.

'Am I, your father, not best placed to secure the welfare of my son?'

Why should I ever know my father, if he is a villain? My heart is satisfied with a mother.

Papa led the men out and returned while Mr Hough was assisting me into my without-door clothes.

'That is better, William. Now make haste. The carriage is waiting.'

'Please, Papa, I feel sick,' I say, making one last attempt to escape. 'I have gripes in my stomach.'

'Nonsense. It is just wind. Have you drunk some milk?'

'I feel sick.'

'Not when we add a drop of this to it.' He takes out his

hip flask and pours a nip of rum into my glass. 'Now get it down you!'

'He is thirteen years old!' Mr Hough says.

'So? Is not rum meted out to the boys on board ship before combat? If it does them no harm when face to face with death, what harm can it do William?'

'But he is not face to face with death, unless you insist on placing him in its path. He does not need an intoxicant; he needs his bed.'

'I am so tired.'

'Take care, Mr Hough. William was never refractory before. I blame you for putting ideas in his head.'

'I am his tutor. It is my duty to put ideas in his head.'

'Do not bandy words with me, sir!' Papa roars so loudly that a supernumerary glances through the door and promptly retreats.

'See, I am drinking it,' I say, taking a gulp and gagging.

'If you have a care for nothing else, think of the receipts,' Mr Hough says. 'The audience will soon fall off if his performances are impaired.'

'I am thinking of the receipts! Lady Abercorn is a leader of fashion, an arbiter of taste. He cannot afford to offend her . . . any more than you can afford to offend me.'

'I feel much better now. I am ready to go,' I interject, desperate to prevent discord. It alarms me when Papa quarrels with Mama, yet, in despite of the slap that is seared on my memory, I am certain that he would never hurt a lady. But men fight one another, like Hamlet and Laertes. Papa is an expert fencer and Mr Hough so puny. It is curious to feel as protective of my tutor as he does of me.

Pressing his advantage, Papa hands me two of the strengthening pills, which both Mama and Mr Hough condemn, and I swallow them without demur. We quit the theatre, passing the guards who hold the well-wishers at bay. I doff my hat as regularly as one of Mr Merlin's automata and pick up a posy that lands at my feet as I enter the carriage. We make our way down the Strand, through Charing Cross and up to Grosvenor Square, arriving at Lady Abercorn's, where we are ushered into the hall.

I frequented so many great houses, and usually so late at night, that I am no more able to distinguish them than I am the subsidiary players in *Hamlet*. I cannot recall whether the grand staircase here contained one flight of steps or two, whether it rose up to the roof or broke off more modestly on the first floor, whether the balustrades were wood or gilt, the ceilings plaster or paint, the columns white or mottled, and the plinths crowned with urns of flowers or the nymphs and goddesses who offered me an anatomy lesson in marble. Whatever the detail, the overall picture is dazzling and, as we mount the stairs, it is animated by bustling footmen in red-and-blue livery, bearing trays of brandy punch. We reach the drawing room, where the raucous chatter is relieved by the notes of a pianoforte. In a voice as resonant as Mr Kemble's, the major-domo announces our names or, rather, two names and a sobriquet: 'The Young Roscius, Mr Betty and Mr Hough.' All at once the din ceases and is replaced by a burst of applause. I am set to perform but, with no prepared lines or gestures, I am far more timorous than ever I am on the stage.

Lady Abercorn approaches me, and hers is the first of the many powdered bosoms into which I am pressed. As I am ruffled and tousled and squeezed and chucked and patted and prodded, I struggle to maintain the permanent smile that Papa has enjoined. One woman, whose slavering jowls suggest that she might be serious, pinches my cheek and declares that she would like to eat me. Were any of my fellow players in the vicinity, I trust that they would be more indulgent to my request not to be touched.

'May I steal Master Betty from you?' Lady Abercorn asks Papa.

'We are all your humble servants, ma'am. What is mine is yours.' I am as yet unversed in such gallantries but, from Lady Abercorn's strained expression, I suspect that Papa's is not to her taste. She leads me through the room, whispering that a very important personage wishes to compliment me. I prepare myself for the Prince of Wales, but the man leaning against the chimney-piece, in conversation with our host, is as emaciated as the prince is corpulent and as pale as he is florid.

'Prime Minister, may I present Master Betty? William meet William,' she adds, lightening her tone more easily than my father. I bow, as Mr Pitt fixes me with a kindly but searching gaze.

'Master Betty, I shall have to charge you for my laundress. I wept so copiously during your performance that my handkerchief is quite sodden. See!' He takes out the square which, being white, looks the same wet or dry.

'Mr Hough takes care of my money, sir.' Mr Pitt's laugh is echoed by those who overhear our exchange, and I find myself hailed as a wit.

'So he should. A talent such as yours should not concern itself with humdrum matters. Leave that to moilers and toilers like – what was the man's name?'

'Hough,' Lord Abercorn replies.

'Mr Hough and me. How do you do it? How does one so young convey the truth that it takes the rest of us a lifetime to learn:

"How weary, stale, flat, and unprofitable
Seem to me all the uses of this world!"?'
'Shakespeare wrote the words, sir,' I reply.
'But you gave them such perfect voice: "Why it appeareth
nothing to me but a foul and pestilential congregation of
vapours."'
'Enough, William,' Lord Abercorn says. 'You will distress the boy.'
'Nonsense. He is strong. "There is special providence in
the fall of a sparrow . . ." He is strong.' He breaks off and
stares intently at his glass, which Lord Abercorn summons
a footman to fill, while his wife whisks me away to circuit
her guests. An elderly lady, with a bosom as crinkled as
her bodice, gathers me into her arms and declares that my
return to plant a kiss on Ophelia's brow, after condemning
her to the nunnery, is the most telling point she has ever
seen on any stage. A young man, with a moustache like two
question marks punctuating his cheeks, commends me on
my precocious understanding of the female sex. When I
look blank, he quotes: 'Frailty, thy name is woman!' and
receives a rap on the knuckles from his companion's fan.
Lady Abercorn introduces me to a wizened gentleman, who
has long exceeded the psalmist's span but who shakes my
hand with a vigour that belies his years.

'What a joy to see Hamlet jumping into the grave!
Kemble simply stares at it as if he fears that he will never be
able to climb out again.'

'I hear he is trying to have a bill brought in banning any
actor under the age of twenty-one,' Lady Abercorn says.

'He will have to buy himself a seat first,' the old man
says. 'No one else will propose it.'

They both laugh, oblivious of the horror that the prospect

has evoked in me. Lady Abercorn leads me towards a couple deep in conversation, only to shrink back on seeing that it is my father and a young woman, whose voice, hair, lips and dress combine to create an impression of softness, which is offset only by the glitter of her jewels. Not sharing our hostess's delicacy, she enthuses about my beauty, my charms and my performance.

'But Clarinda, you did not attend the play,' Lady Abercorn says sternly.

'So?' she replies. 'I have heard so much about it that I feel as though I did.'

Lady Abercorn draws me away and into the path of a heavyset man with a bald pate, as shiny and smooth as a banister, and a smattering of crumbs on his chin. 'I shall be back, Sir Peter, but first I have to deliver the Young Roscius to his tutor. He is due to recite.'

'Forgive me, dear lady, but you must grant me a word with our guest of honour.'

I edge towards him. Notwithstanding his unprepossessing appearance, I welcome any opportunity for delay.

'Yes, of course, but just the one.'

'Ask anyone here and they will tell you that I am the exemplar . . . the epitome . . . the paragon of plain speaking. I was full of admiration – no one more so – for your performance tonight, but I beseech you not to repeat it.'

'No?'

'The part . . . the play is unworthy of you. Oh, it begins well enough. The first two acts are creditably done. Hamlet's mourning for his father, his resentment of his mother's marriage, his apprehension at the ghost. After which it descends into lamentable farce and moral confusion. His playing the fool, his mockery of Polonius, all the idle talk.

Camels and whales: buffoonery! Mere buffoonery! To say nothing of the bawdry with Ophelia.'

'What is bawdry?'

'See what you have started, Sir Peter?' Lady Abercorn says. 'It is nothing to trouble you now, William.'

'Exactly,' Sir Peter says. 'You must preserve the innocence we all revere. You should play parts only of nobility and candour.'

'But I am an actor.'

'You are the Young Roscius!'

My Hamlet was on every tongue. Mr Fox, who opposed Mr Pitt in Parliament, dined me at his club and avowed that my impersonation was finer than Garrick's. Mr Sheridan, who was of the company, added that it was certainly more remunerative, but as ever it was hard to know quite what he meant. Years later, during one of our colloquies at Christ's, Harness told me that his schoolfriend Byron, whose poem of *Childe Harold* beguiled me at Pyms Farm this summer, saw the performance twice and rhapsodized over it.

One week I played the part at Covent Garden and the next at Drury Lane, which Mr Fox likened to moving from the Whig to the Tory benches and back again in the same session, prompting a furtive look from Mr Sheridan, whose machinations were the cause of my divided loyalties. I grew so weary that sometimes in the side-wing I had to check my costume to know whether I were in Denmark, Italy or Peru. Whatever I may have said in the past, I now feared that I would die if I were to remain a player. I begged for a respite but was advised of my duty. Papa, whose arguments were always compelling, pointed out that the country was at war and there were boys of my age and younger under enemy fire, who could not retire to their camps or cabins at will.

'Besides, they will proceed against me if you fail to fulfil your engagement. Do you wish to see your poor Papa thrown into the Clink?'

'For pity's sake!' said Mr Hough, who stood beside us in the dressing room, his expression shifting from anxiety to scorn.

'You have no conception, William, of the expenses I have sustained in securing your position,' Papa said, ignoring him. 'The lodgings, the carriages, the servants, the clothes, the gifts for your friends and admirers. The money no sooner comes in than it disappears.'

'Yes,' Mr Hough said. 'On the faro tables at Boodle's. On jewels that I have yet to see adorning Mrs Betty.'

'May I remind you, sir, that you are in my employ?'

'If you continue to work him like this, there will be no employ.'

'I feel better now,' I interject swiftly. 'I am ready to dress.'

'Of course you are. You are young and strong. Here, take this glass of water and another two of Papa's restorative pills. Wait and see. Tonight you will give your finest performance yet.'

'I must protest,' Mr Hough said.

'No,' Papa replied. 'That is precisely what you must not do. You must keep silent! Look at him. He is thirteen years old.'

'I shall be fourteen in September.'

'Exactly. Have you seen how he has grown during the past year?'

'Which is good, is it not, Papa? I shall no longer need the lifts in my shoes. No one will be able to complain that I look smaller than the other actors.'

'Of course it is not good,' Papa said, turning from Mr Hough to me. 'Do you think they will still want you when your youthful charms have faded? Look, there is already down on your upper lip!' He grabbed my face and I feared that he would pull out the hairs one by one, but he disengaged his hand and let out a sigh midway between disgust and despair. 'You will have plenty of time to rest when they have no more use for you. Soon you will be imploring me: "Papa, please find me a theatre where I can act!"' He squeaked, in mimicry and frustration. 'Until then, we must profit from what we can. So make haste and put on your costume. Mr Hough can help. At least that is one task he never refuses.'

Looking back, I am as dismayed by his lack of faith in me as by the accuracy of his prediction. All at once the theatre feels as oppressive as a tread-wheel, and I hurry out and back to my lodgings. I sit down with Miss Edgeworth's *The Absentee*, which Mama slipped into my valise when I left home, declaring that I would find much that was familiar in its twin societies of Irish country folk and London fashionists. As I plough through its pages (my slow progress prompted more by the shooting in my head than any perplexities in the prose), I suspect that she had a secondary reason for selecting the story of an honourable father, encumbered with debts incurred through no fault of his own. But I am not of a mind to pursue it and, closing the book, I proceed to Sawyer's where, in a spirit of defiance (although of whom or what I cannot say), I eat a dish of stewed oysters, a lobster, a slice of pickled salmon and an apple pie.

Feeling uncomfortably full, I take a promenade along the Strand. The chill air matches my mood and I consider a companionable visit to the Coal Hole, but I fear that any player of worth will be gainfully occupied, and I will be left with those untroubled by the call boy all season. Besides, as I pass a young officer and his lady gazing at the prints in Ackermann's window, his bicorne and her bonnet almost touching, I realise that I crave more intimate companionship.

A chaste exchange of kisses with Letty apart, I have shared greater intimacies with rheumy-eyed duchesses than with girls of my own age. I feel a desperate need to prove my mettle in the chamber as well as on the stage. Quelling my distaste for the pecuniary stamp of such relations, I approach one of the bagnios in the piazza, until the fear of a chance encounter when Mama and Marianne arrive in town tomorrow stops me in my tracks.

I head down Long Acre, where I hail a link boy, one of a breed reputed to be steeped in the practice of vice. Doubling his farthing fee, I order him to light my way to St Giles. Asked if I have any particular address in mind, I answer faintly that I seek somewhere I might enjoy an hour's conversation with an accommodating young woman. Reclaiming the brazenness I displayed as Osmond, I elaborate: 'A doxy who would not object to a small emolument in return for the pleasure of her company.' He proposes to conduct me to Chick Lane, where I will be sure to find everything from a threepenny upright to a ten-year-old dell. Each step I take increases my trepidation but, determined not to lose heart, I follow him to the designated street, where he quits me, the flicker of his torch replaced by thick fog and louring shadows. Thin shafts of light from forbidding doorways and the sinister glint of shuttered windows are all that relieve the gloom.

'Lost, sweetheart?' One of the shadows transmutes into

a woman, her age and face indeterminate but her accent distinctively northern.

'No, not at all, miss, thank you,' I reply, trusting that my vision will clear before I am obliged to commit myself.

'It ain't half nippy out here. What say you and I take a pot of beer together in the Angel?' My hesitation emboldens her and, hooking her arm through mine, she draws me down the street to a heavy door, which opens to reveal a set of steep and slippery steps and a crowded tavern. Our arrival causes so little stir that I realise it must be a familiar resort for such dealings. I am reassured to find that, while her face is weatherworn and her teeth green, she is no younger than sixteen and no older than twenty-five. I give her sixpence for the beer and take a seat on a bench, where condensation from the low ceiling drips on my neck. She returns, having pocketed the change, and pours us both a tankard. 'Here's to luck!' she says and quaffs so heartily that I turn my sip into a slurp.

'You're a fair way from home, I'll wager,' she says, refilling her tankard.

'How about you?' I ask. 'Unless I am much mistaken, you come from Manchester.'

'Not far off. Rochdale. Don't s'pose you know it?'

'Does it have a theatre?'

'I can't rightly say. What's it to you?'

'Nothing.'

'I can see I got me a card.'

'So what are you doing here?'

'Hoping to find me a handsome-looking, generous gentleman,' she replies, simpering.

'Well you have found one,' I say, relaxing into the role of rake. 'What I meant was: what are you doing in London?'

'Seeking my fortune, what else?' She beckons me close, the beer fumes failing to mask the staleness of her breath. 'I hooked it when I was ten (see, I've kept a tally of my years, even if no one else has). I was a scavenger in the mill. Scrabbling about under the looms to pick off the scraps. I saw girls who were crushed by the cogs and the pulleys. I was lucky; I got away with just two fingers.' She holds up a mutilated hand. 'Still, it can be handy in my line of work. Handy, see?' She cackles, and I try not to shudder. 'I made it down to London barefoot.'

'The whole way?'

'Barefoot and shank's nag. They didn't give us no shoes, to stop us from hooking it. But nothing stopped me. I wanted to be a lady's maid. Like Clara at Mrs Lumsden's – she was the missus at the mill. When I got here, my guts crying out, near done for, I met this fine lady, see, and I thought I'd lucked it. She said she'd get me a position in a fine house, with fine clothes. She got me a position all right, but the house was Mrs Cummins' in Half Moon Street. All scrubbed up, I was a pretty child. You don't ever want to be a pretty child, sir.' I feel my heart race. 'She hawked my maidenhead like a drover at the market cross. Turned out to be worth a tidy penny. What's that they say: you can't miss summat you don't know you have? I'm not sure that's true, sir. Not sure at all.'

Alarmed by her melancholy, I give her sixpence for another pot of beer. When she returns, the smile on her face like a darn in a stocking, I feel a deep compulsion to confide in her, if only to dissociate myself from the men who had bid to deflower her. 'I also came to London as a child.'

'You too?' she replies, the drink enlivening her.

'I was an actor at Drury Lane and Covent Garden. I was known as the Young Roscius.' I have no idea why, having striven so hard to shake off my past, I should now boast of it and to one to whom it must be a matter of indifference.

'You're the Young Roscius?' I nod. 'Bugger my eyes, you've bellied!'

'Yes,' I say, laughing. With this woman, I have no need to explain myself. 'Like you, I am no longer a pretty child.'

'I saw you once. Just once. But I won't never forget it.'

'Where?'

'At the playhouse. On quiet nights, Mrs Cummins used to send us girls to tout for culls. Half-price entrance after nine.'

'At the end of the third act.'

'Some gentlemen always managed to slip out. But not that night. I walked up and down the corridor and in and out of the coffee rooms and not a body turned up. Seeing there was nothing doing, I crept into the gallery and watched the play. It was special, like nothing else I ever saw. You wore a skirt.'

'Then it must have been Norval.'

'No, it was a skirt. You had two swords, one in both hands. You killed someone, but it was out of sight.'

'The villain, Glenalvon.'

'Then you came back to your mother. But you were wounded, about to die. You spoke to her, the most beautiful words . . . the most beautiful voice I ever heard. You were so beautiful. It was like nothing else mattered: nothing that had been done to me; nothing I done. Just to know there was beauty like that in the world was enough. You were small but fearless. I'd have been scared half to death in front of all those people. You stared straight at them.'

'It was only polite.'

'The other actors seemed like they were speaking among themselves. But you were speaking to us . . . no, to me. You took me somewhere – not to a better time; I ain't never known a better time. But to a time when everything will be better.'

'I hope so. Truly.'

'And now you're just like all the rest. Itching to wind your way up cock alley.'

'I am not like all the rest!'

'No, course not. Don't mind me. What do I know? A common trull!'

'I am not like all the rest. Not at all. Here, take this.' I hand her a crown. 'I have to go.'

'But you have paid—'

'And you have given. This was not what I came for, not what I was expecting. But nothing you said could have meant more. I wish . . . I wish . . .'

I cannot say what I wish, but I know that preserving her ideal is more precious to me than quenching my desire. I leave the tavern and make my way back to my lodgings, my virtue, if not hers, intact.

6

I slip the seal sheepishly into my pocket. I cannot banish the thought of Harkness likening me to a Papist, who places his faith in relics and rosaries rather than in the Bible and Prayer Book. But after the distressing memories evoked by my return to London, I sent word to Mama to bring it with her. If it is a relic of anything, it is of my fame.

It was presented to me by William Smith, a member of Garrick's company, who had been numbered among his particular friends. On his deathbed, the great man gave him a seal imprinted with his likeness, instructing him to pass it on, should he ever find a player whom he judged to be his worthy successor, one who 'acted from Nature and from feeling.'

After twenty-five years, Mr Smith claimed to have abandoned hope of fulfilling his charge until, prevailed upon by his wife, he came to see my Selim. I recollect his calling on me in my dressing room, but as ever there was a dreadful crush, and I fear that Papa, with his unswerving devotion to my advancement, may have ignored him in favour of more illustrious visitors. He took my hand and, overcome by sentiment, pressed it to his breast. To the best of my remembrance, he spoke but little. Then a few days later, a package arrived at our lodgings containing the seal and a dedicatory verse, which has vanished along with most of the other poems sent to me, either mislaid on our various travels or else discarded by Papa in favour of more lucrative tributes. According to several of the memoirists – who appear to have eavesdropped on my most private conversations – I gazed at the seal and, quoting Hamlet, stated that I would wear it in my heart's core.

In this memoir, I shall speak only in my own words and not those fed to me by a tutor, however well-disposed.

The next event I must record is the arrival of Mama and Marianne on Monday evening, in readiness for my return to Covent Garden on Friday. I have secured them rooms with Mrs Stirling and, indeed, exchanged mine with Marianne, in order that she might enjoy the prospect of the piazza. It is her first visit to the metropolis since she was a babe in arms eight years ago, and she is as thrilled by the hurry-scurry in the shops and the streets as by the spectacle of a liveried blackamoor on the footboard of a carriage. Her heart melts at the sight of the mutilated soldiers begging for alms, and she would ruin us if Mama did not intervene. She is determined to see all the attractions, and so yesterday morning, while I was at the second partial rehearsal, Mama took her to St Paul's, the Guildhall and the Monument to the Great Fire, and then in the afternoon to Mr Barker's Panorama in Leicester Place. She walked round and round the main display, craning her neck to take in the multifarious views of the bay of Messina, its verisimilitude, according to Mama, demonstrating the futility of foreign travel. Then she ran headlong down two flights of stairs and was sick.

With no calls on my time until the group rehearsal tomorrow, I offer to take Marianne to St James, to see the Park and some of the great houses whose doors had once been open to me and will, I trust, soon be so again. Mama, who never cared for the world of the bon ton, declines to accompany us. In despite of my pleas, she had refused to attend the receptions to which I was invited in my youth, declaring that she had nothing to wear ('You will be the most beautiful lady there,' I countered) or nothing to say ('Your stories are better than anyone's,') or, to clinch the matter, that she had to look after the baby. 'Besides,' she told me, 'you will have Papa and Mr Hough.' Now I wonder whether Papa, keen to pursue his own interests, persuaded her to stay away.

As I leave her to her correspondence, I promise not to exhaust my little sister, whereupon she laughingly warns me that Marianne has more endurance than the two of us combined. With a child in my charge, I am newly aware of the perils of the crowd and insist on her holding on to me as we stroll down the Strand. I feel her grip tense at the sound of Chunee's trumpeting. It slackens when I explain that he is an elephant, not a monster, but she continues to fret about his confinement, unconvinced by my assurance that he is the most fortunate elephant in history, having lately appeared on the Covent Garden stage.

'Not everything is best on your stupid stage!'

We traverse Charing Cross, where the throng thickens. At one corner, a mountebank diverts spectators while his quack dispenses remedies and, at another, a trick-of-the-loop man gulls the credulous of their coin. We linger outside the Golden Cross to watch a hurdy-gurdy player and his monkey, but my sister is more intrigued by a girl, younger – or, at any rate, slighter – than herself, bareheaded, unshod and clad in a ragged smock, who stands by the door, selling matches. Tuppence the poorer, we make our way down Pall Mall and into the path of two begrimed boys, shouting 'Sweep for the soot!' as they scuttle around their masters, who keep them matchstick-thin to expedite their ascent of the flues. We reach the colonnade of Carlton House and peer at the guards marching up and down before the gates. Sensing Marianne's excitement, I recount how I was received there on several occasions.

'What is it like inside?' she asks.

'Fairyland. I forget exactly; it was a long time ago.'

'You always say that. Try, you must try!'

'We were taken into a room that was all blue – the walls, the ceiling and the carpet. I thought that we would wait there for the Prince, but we were met by a major domo, who led us into another room that was all rose, with only a faint billowing in the curtains to distinguish them from the walls. Then we went through a door like a looking glass into a third room, which was a perfect circle, hung with drapes – I think they were blue too – so that it felt as if we were in a tent, equipped for an eastern potentate like Osman, whom you will see in the play on Friday. Oh yes, there was a frieze of naked boys festooned with fruit and foliage.'

'Was it rude?'

'It was gold.'

'What else?' She pulls a face. 'Tell me!' Fearful of attracting an audience, I steer her to a quieter spot.

'There was a conservatory fashioned like a church, the windows ornamented with coats of arms, like the ones in the transept of St Martin's. One for each king. But the best room of all was Chinese. It was coloured red, with black and gold pagodas on the walls and a huge dragon on the ceiling.'

'Was it breathing fire?'

'Both from its nostrils and its mouth. The carpet was

patterned with the signs of the zodiac – no, they may have been on the ceiling too! In its centre was a scene of Chinese junks in harbour. I remember that Papa was angry when I refused to walk on it. He said that the Prince would take me for a bumpkin, who had never seen an elegant carpet before. No more I had. Not one like that.'

'Is that where you met the Prince?'

'Maybe, or maybe he took us in to show us. He was very proud of everything.'

'Was he wearing a crown?'

'Yes and carrying an orb and sceptre! No, of course not. Do you wear a hat in the house?'

'How I hate you! What was he like?' Her question gives me pause.

'I cannot altogether say. Cordial but remote . . . kindly but indifferent. It felt as though he were addressing me from a great height, and not just because he was so much taller. He called me "My cousin of Denmark."'

'What for?'

'I read you the *Tales from Shakespeare*. Prince Hamlet.'

'Oh, the play!'

'He told me how much he admired actors, yet he teased them. He imitated Mr Kemble's enunciations. His "airs and graces" . . . not the ones he assumed – if, indeed, he did – but the way he drew out the words. "Aaaaaiiiiirrrrrsssss and grrrrraaaaaccccceeeeessss."' Marianne giggles. 'He looked disappointed when I failed to laugh as loudly as Papa. He did not seem to be comfortable talking to boys. Or maybe it was just to me. But he knew what presents to give them!'

'Presents?'

'I thought that would make you take note. He gave me a coach and four, emblazoned with his coat of arms.'

'For your fort?'

'No, ninny! For real. To ride in around town.'

'Where is it now? What happened to the horses?'

'I have no idea.' Until I embarked on this tour, I might have supposed that the Prince had requested the coach back or else that Papa had returned it when we left London. Given my recent recollections, however, I suspect that he may have sold it, profiting by its royal provenance. But it would not do to disillusion Marianne, who remains deeply affected by his death.

'Did you go for drives in the park?'

'Plenty. Although not in my own carriage. I never had the chance. I received so many invitations from great ladies.'

'But you were just a boy!'

'No, I was a trophy. They wanted to show me off, along with their latest gown or hat or coiffure. One day it would be Lady Cholmondeley, the next Lady Abercorn or Lady Foster or the Duchess of Devonshire. Not that it made much difference. We sat opposite each other in the vis-à-vis.'

'What a silly name!'

'It is French for face to face.'

'Miss Merry says that no one should talk French while we are at war.'

'Then we sat opposite each other in the middle of nowhere.'

'Who is the ninny now?' she asks, smacking my arm.

'I am, I admit it. Then and now. They would address me at length and it was often hard to discern a question beneath all the courtesies. But whatever my response, no matter how short or tentative, they would profess to find it uncommonly droll. Papa and Mr Hough had hammered into me that I had to conduct myself as correctly as if I were on the stage. And Hyde Park at five o'clock was like a stage. A cavalcade of carriages and horsemen circled the Ring. The difference was that they were actual generals and ministers and lords and ladies and sometimes even the Prince. He drove himself in his curricle, with his groom at his side. For all that he was fat, he was an expert whip.'

'I shall never marry somebody fat. Oh, I did not mean—'

'I am your brother, so you are in no danger,' I reply, to relieve her embarrassment. 'Besides, who says anyone will ask you?' She sticks out her tongue. 'I rest my case. Come along!' I clasp her hand and stride down the pavement, as eager to escape my memories as to reach the park. She runs towards the lake, flinging herself on the grass, to the marked disapproval of a pair of nursemaids who whisk away their charges.

We amble to Duck Island to see the pelicans. I parry the inevitable 'Why is it not called Pelican Island?' with a 'Why are you not called Goose?' She swallows her indignation in the excitement of seeing a scoop of three: two swimming and a third preening itself in the reeds. Easily bored, she moves off to watch a milkmaid selling cups of milk, fresh from the cow. Her companion, meanwhile, stands in close conversation with a young soldier, like the clandestine lovers in an afterpiece. Afraid that her natural curiosity will not be confined to the pelicans and the cow, I drag Marianne away, pointing out Buckingham House behind the trees.

'That is the Queen's House.'

'Did you go there too?'

'Never.'

'But the King and Queen came to see you perform?'

'No. People think that they did – and Papa used to claim it, although not in London – but the only time I met them was in the theatre lobby. I was acting at Covent Garden and they were watching the play at Drury Lane. The king expressed the desire to see me, so Mr Sheridan fetched me when I came off the stage. I was all goose-flesh. I knew that the king was mad and was expecting him to babble like Ophelia. But he just looked me up and down as if I were a painting and said he thought that I would be taller.'

'Was that all?'

'His only words. For my part, I thought that he would be grander, like the Prince of Wales.'

Marianne yawns.

'Are you weary?'

'Of course not, silly. Where are we going now?'

I lead the way towards Piccadilly, feeling a pang as we pass Spencer House. It was there, in a room with pillars shaped like palm trees and statues in the attitude of Lady Randolph pleading for her son, that I attended one of my most lavish receptions. I had to sit on a golden chair, while a lady dressed as Britannia, holding a trident and shield as if on a coin, recited an ode in my honour. Unlike the others, it has survived, since it was published in the next morning's papers and transcribed by the memoirists. So, with both a blush and a sense of pride, I include it here:

Since days of yore,
O'er Britain's shore
I e'er have cast mine eye,
To guard her laws,
Uphold her cause,
And guide her destiny.

Her history bold on every page
Is my delight to read,
And on the glory of her stage
My heart doth ever feed.
And so in this o'erclouded hour
With danger ever near,
A hero have I sent with power
Each loyal heart to cheer.
A little child, an angel fair,
Graced with the Muses' fire,
A prodigy beyond compare
His country to inspire.
And when at last this war with France
Is gloriously won,
The soldiers too will have the chance
To cheer my favourite son.
And none will clap as loud as they,
Their wounds they count at naught.
Their joy to see Young Roscius play
Worth every fight they fought.

I squirmed when Britannia kissed me and again when
she pressed a crown of laurel leaves on my head. It scratched
and I longed to take it off, but Papa, who called me 'a
monster of ingratitude' (a phrase that is steadily weaving
itself into my cognizance), made me wear it all night. As
ever, the guests plied me with questions, which felt more
like excuses to hear themselves talk.

'Were you content with the performance tonight?'
'Why? Did I do something wrong?'
'You excelled yourself. The boxes were awash with tears.'
'I hope that they laughed at the clowns.'

A ruffle of my hair or a squeeze of my arm, and one interrogator departed, to be replaced by another.

'When you play Hamlet, are you in your right senses or transported into a temporary distraction?'

'If I were not fully sensible, how would I remember all the lines?'

Ruffle ruffle, squeeze squeeze: the hands changed but the torment continued.

'Which of your roles do you prefer?'

'Whichever one I am playing.' I parroted the answer with which I had been primed.

'Which do you think that you most succeed in?'

'It is not for me to say. Mr Hough tells me my faults.'

'Do you study all your attitudes from antiquity?'

'No, only in the morning.'

There were parties on the days when I was playing and parties on the days when I was not. The locations shifted, from Cleveland House to Devonshire House to Coventry House to Abercorn House, but the company remained the same. The pills and acrid-tasting milk fed to me by Papa staved off my exhaustion, yet I struggled to reconcile the heaviness of my head, and the voices that boomed at me as in an empty church, with his insistence that I was the 'most favoured boy alive'. As I yearned to escape, envying the ladies who were carried out in a swoon at my performances, I could only think that his charge was just. I was indeed a monster of ingratitude.

I yearn once again to escape and usher Marianne up St James's Street, where White's and Brook's clubs face each other across the street, much like their members across the floor of the House of Commons. I baulk at the sight of Boodle's, to which Papa was introduced by the Bowbearer of the Forest of Bowland (I cannot say why, but I find it easier to refer to his title than his name). It was last week in my dressing room that I recalled the club for the first time in years. Along with it came the memory of late-night quarrels, when Mama accused Papa of gambling away my receipts and the family's future. Why did the Bowbearer encourage him? No one as cultivated as he could have welcomed Papa's company. Was it sheer devilry that made him play on his weakness? Or did he have a more sinister motive for seeking to drive him into his debt?

Having no way – and no wish – to answer, I join Marianne, who is inspecting the array of perfumes in the apothecary's window next door. She gazes at me with a plea that she is reluctant to voice. Amused by her diffidence and eager to shake off the air of covert desperation that emanates from Boodle's, I lead her into the shop and treat her to a bottle of Dr Harris' lavender water, which the proprietor assures me is the most suitable fragrance for a young girl. To conclude the excursion, I guide her across Piccadilly to Berkeley Square and buy us each an ice at Gunter's: violet and jasmine for her; gruyère and mint for me. We take a seat by the window and watch the ladies nibbling ices and sweetmeats without descending from their carriages, while their beaux stand beside them beneath a canopy of maple leaves.

'If you had kept the prince's coach, we could join them,' Marianne says, entranced by the spectacle.

'I doubt that many of them are brother and sister.'

'Ugh!' Marianne retorts, gobbling her ice.

We make our way back to Henrietta Street, where Marianne regales Mama with a breathless account of princes, pelicans and perfumes. Mama's insistence that any fragrance is improper for a girl of eight puts Marianne into such a pet that I precipitate my departure for the theatre and our sole group rehearsal of *Barbarossa*, which, in despite of Mrs Powell's gout, proceeds so happily that, in my third act reunion with Zaphira, I have to remember to save my powers for the performance. I return to the lodgings, to find peace restored after Mama's concession that Marianne may wear the scent at home, when there is no company. But later that evening, sitting beside her to watch Mr Grimaldi in the pantomime, I detect a pungent odour of lavender and trust that Mama is sniffing her vinaigrette.

I wonder whether, had I first seen Mr Grimaldi rather than Mrs Siddons in Belfast all those years ago, I would have set my heart on becoming a clown. Never before have I sat in such a rapt house. Unlike other players, he has no problem in conveying his expressions to the back of the shilling gallery. Although the audience there are too distant to catch his rolled eyes, dropped jaw and sidelong glances, they can still relish his singular physiognomy: the blue coxcomb, red spangled cheeks and bright scarlet mouth in a permanent gape of delight. Marianne and I dispute our preferred scenes: mine being when he dresses as a hussar, turning coal scuttles into boots, with horseshoes on the heels and candlesticks as spurs, clattering noisily as he ridicules foreign foppery; hers being when he rides to hounds on a giant carthorse, wearing a huge peaked cap and wielding an elongated whip, pursuing Pantaloon on a minute pony.

'I wish that you would be in a pantomime, William,' she says dreamily.

'Nonsense! William is an actor of gravity,' Mama interjects, reminding me of the old stager (was it in town or the country?), whose proud boast was that he had never blackened his face, played in a farce or risen from a trap.

During the entr'acte a shrunken old man enters our box. He makes his bow with all the elegance of a practised courtier, yet his clothes are rumpled and shabby. I am in agonies of confusion until Mama comes to my rescue. 'Mr Northcote, a pleasure!'

'Madam.' He kisses her hand. 'Master Betty.' He extends his hand to me.

'It is Mr Betty now,' Mama says.

'Of course, of course,' he replies and wrings my hand more robustly, as if to redress the error.

'This is my sister, Marianne,' I say, as she stares sullenly at the intruder. 'Mr Northcote painted me. You have seen the picture in the hall at Pyms.'

'Where you stand on the mountain with the spear?'

'No,' I say, wincing, as she alludes to my portrait as Norval by Mr Opie, Mr Northcote's great rival. 'Where I am in a temple before an altar to Shakespeare.'

'I like the other one better.'

'Marianne!' Mama exclaims.

'Pray, do not distress yourself, madam,' Mr Northcote says. 'We painters must develop the hide of an elephant.'

'Like players,' I say, struck by thoughts of Chunee, who proved to be so intractable that, after a handful of performances, he was withdrawn from the stage and sold to Pidcock's.

'I see that plain speaking is a family trait. Have you forgotten, Mr Betty, how violently you objected to the picture?'

'I did?'

'Expressly to the way you were apparelled.'

'I am mortified.'

'You were a boy.'

I must have passed the picture ten times a day when I traversed the hall but had forgotten the circumstances of its painting. He portrayed me as Hamlet in a temple to Shakespeare, with a bowl of incense burning by my side. I had visited just such a temple when staying with the Duke and Mrs Jordan at Bushy. It had been built by their neighbour, Garrick, and was now tended by his widow, who was most welcoming to me, even while dismissing my alleged resemblance to her husband.

We entered the temple through an underground grotto, lit, according to the Duke, by five hundred lanterns, although I gave up the count after fifty. In the place of honour was a statue of Shakespeare, for which the Duke said that Garrick himself had posed, although his widow dismissed that resemblance too. I sat on a chair, which the Duke assured me had been Shakespeare's own, but which Mrs Garrick maintained had been carved after his death from a mulberry tree in his garden. I donned Shakespeare's signet ring and pretended it was stuck to my finger, until the Duke, remarking Mrs Garrick's unease, picked up a dagger, which had also belonged to Shakespeare, and proposed to cut it off.

I have no notion whether Mr Northcote had Garrick's temple in mind. The Duke could certainly have told him of my visit when he accompanied me to the sittings. I was prepared to license his truncating the statue to a bust, but not his dressing me as Hamlet. I complained that people would suppose that I walked abroad in my costume rather than ordinary, without-doors attire.

'Your brother is the most fidgety subject I have ever painted,' Mr Northcote says to Marianne, who for some reason he is seeking to charm. 'And that includes the horses.' She chuckles. 'He is also the most profitable. The moment that they heard he was frequenting my workroom, a dozen ladies sent requests for their portraits, just so that they could catch a glimpse of him on the stairs.'

'Do not remind me! I had to be the young gallant off the stage as well as on, allowing myself to be petted and kissed, my cheeks stroked and my hair mussed.'

'From what I hear, other actresses have to contend with worse,' Mr Northcote says.

'I was not an actress; I was a boy!'

'Of course. Forgive me! A slip of the tongue.'

'William, take care. You are making a spectacle of yourself,' Mama says, as heads turn towards us. At that moment the orchestra strikes up and Mr Northcote returns to his seat for the second act, but not before securing my promise that, after escorting Mama and Marianne back to the lodgings, I will join him for a bowl of punch at the Shakespeare's Head. I arrive to find him snugly installed beside the fire. A pot-boy, in a greasy shirt, brings me a plate of comfits, as Mr Northcote pours me a cup of wine. We sit in companionable silence, which he is the first to break.

'I heard that you were to become a parson.'

'So I was. Perhaps one day I will play Cardinal Wolsey. That would please my father. At least . . .'

'It would please your friends, who are eager to see you add to your list of triumphs.'

'Which friends? There are precious few names in the box keeper's book.'

'You must be patient. Times have changed; you have changed. In your youth, you were a phenomenon: a prodigy. Now you have it in you to be the first actor in the land.'

— 141 —

'Are you mocking me?'

'By no means. I speak from the heart.' I feel a tingling in my eyelids and cough in an attempt to attribute it to his pipe. 'You played as if privy to truths hidden from the rest of us. You had an understanding so far beyond your years that it could only have come from the gods.'

'You will unman me,' I say, no longer attempting to conceal my emotion.

'As you did all of us . . . I mean the men. You imbued your playing with a melancholy that touched my very core. I used to wonder whether there were some secret sadness in your life.'

'None whatsoever. I have revisited many forgotten scenes since I made my return – scenes from my own life that is, not my characters' – but I know that I would have remembered anything of import. I was a happy child: a parlour child in my mother's phrase, since she taught me herself rather than sending me to school. I was sad when my pug dog died and when I had to leave my pony in Ballynahinch, but that was no secret.'

'The prize for me was your Hamlet. Your youth and grace combined to create a prince who was prey, not just to Claudius' villainy, but to time itself. Then there was Romeo, and Norval of course – even if Opie did get to paint him!' He laughs. 'And Selim.'

'There still is – is, not was. I shall be Selim again on Friday.'

'And I shall be there to cheer you on. It is true that I preferred you in the noble, romantic roles that you endowed with such delicacy of spirit, but to my amazement – and that of the whole town – you reigned supreme in roles of whose passions you could have had no knowledge.'

'You speak of Richard and Osmond?'

'Indeed. You were like a child in one of Mr Blake's poems: innocent and yet with a deep wisdom.'

'I am not familiar with the poems.'

'But your looking glass is. I too studied Richard for my two paintings of the Princes in the Tower. Even Cooke, although far more commanding in the role than Kemble, had moments when he played the Crookback like the wicked squire in the pantomime. But you brought some-thing fresh – a sense that you were ensnared by your own body . . . cheated by Nature and resolved to have your revenge. The tenderness that crept into your wooing of Lady Anne showed the man that you might have been.'

'Mr Hough told me to think of him as Buonaparte. Did you know that he is very short? To countervail which he has set out to conquer the world, butchering many more people than ever Richard did.' As I speak, I recall that Mr Northcote is similarly undersized. Fearing that he might suppose me to intend a general equation of diminution and villainy, I rapidly change tack. 'I know that there were some who objected to my playing such parts, maintaining that I was giving voice to sentiments that debauched me.'

'Their cavils were understandable. As Osmond you were driven to rape and murder in order to feed your depraved appetites. At thirteen, not only were you patently too young to play one who had spent sixteen years racked with guilt for stabbing his brother's wife to death, but Mrs Mountain who played Agnes—'

'Angela.'

'Angela, the ward you threatened to ravish, was three times your age. And yet, while there may have been a want of harmony in the stage picture, there was none in the playing.'

'Mr Hough always said that an actor was not obliged to

experience the passions he portrays, merely to convince the audience that he does. What counts is not what he feels, but what they do.'

'He was a shrewd teacher. It was most injudicious of your father to dispense with his services.'

'I think that he came to recognise that himself, although by then it was too late. They quarrelled, not that there was anything unusual in that. But this time there was no reconcilement. Mr Hough left and I never saw him again.'

'Well, you are Mr Betty now and need no one's instruction. But I come as an emissary from your most ardent champion to invite you to dine tomorrow, on the eve of your first performance.'

'Which champion? Who?'

Faces, painted and powdered, bewigged and bewhiskered, dimpled and pinched, loom before me.

'If you cannot guess, I am not at liberty to enlighten you. But I assure you that you will be most pleasantly surprised. I am charged to obtain your assent, indeed, your pledge to extricate yourself should you be engaged elsewhere.'

'I am quite unoccupied throughout the day. I have been wondering how to spend it and suspect that I shall be obliged to take Marianne on another excursion.'

'If you are truly at leisure, then I would welcome your company on a visit to the Armourers' Hall. I am to inspect the display of my *Richard and Bolingbroke*. The company of Armourers and Braziers (no doubt there is a *Worshipful* in there somewhere) bought it when Mr Boydell's Shakespeare Gallery foundered. You expressed a most gratifying interest in the painting once before.'

I recollect it only dimly, but his fervent endorsement of my work requires me to return the compliment. I accept the invitation with pleasure and, as we part for the night, he promises to call for me at the lodgings at eleven.

He arrives just as the church clock strikes the hour. To my surprise, he refuses to hire a hackney, insisting that the exercise will do us good, a gentler allusion to my girth than those to which I have become accustomed. We make our way down the Strand and Fleet Street through a light drizzle, which grows heavier when we pass St Paul's and turn into Cheapside. But the weather is mild for the time of year, and I have no fear of contracting a chill before the performance.

On reaching the hall, we are escorted across a quadrangle and up the stairs to a landing place lined, unsurprisingly, with suits of ancient armour and weaponry. My attempt to shoulder a matchlock is curtly proscribed by the attendant. His concern for the arms is equalled by his ignorance of the art, as he takes us first into the court room, where the only picture on show is a portrait of a grim-visaged seventeenth century armourer, and then into the dining room where, with Shakespeare his sole guide, he ascribes to Mr Northcote a drab ball scene from *Romeo and Juliet*.

The painter thanks him with remarkable equanimity and moves to examine his own canvas of *Richard and Bolingbroke's Entry into London*: the deposed king disconsolate on a bay horse, and the usurper greeting the crowd from a prancing white one. I praise the richness and passion of the tableau, which is not so much true to life as true to theatre, with the attitudes of the cheering women in the foreground looking as if they had been sketched from a stage box. Mr Northcote, meanwhile, protests at the inferior position of his Richard to the Romeo, as bitterly as a Rosencrantz placed consistently behind Guildenstern.

Leaving word for the Master of the Company, he ushers me out and proposes to walk back by way of Moorfields. As we set off, I recount my previous visit there with Sir George Beaumont, when I watched a man wrestling a horse.

'Who won the day?'

'The man. He held him down by the withers. But his face was torn and bloodied and his arm hung slackly by his side. Sir George gave him a guinea for his mettle. Even so . . .' The sight of a long narrow building behind a well laid-out garden transfixes me. 'What is that?' I ask my companion.

'Bethlem . . . Bedlam . . . The Royal Bethlehem Hospital. It is not somewhere you would wish to enter.'

'But I have done,' I say, as a long-buried memory rises up like a corpse in a flooded field. 'Of course. We were on the way to the hospital, when Sir George spotted the bout and stopped the carriage.'

'I understood that admission to the public had been restricted. Or were all doors open to Master Betty?'

'As far as I recall, Sir George was acquainted with the governor. Yes, it was he who showed us round. Sir George had lately given us a tour of his picture gallery – Papa, Mama and, I think, Mr Hough. He was also eager for us to see these curiosities of flesh and blood. "The inmates are such singular characters. They will be of particular interest to our young hero. Like the finest actors, they offer both moral instruction and diversion." I doubt that he considered the implications of his remark. Please, let us go back by the way we came.'

'We shall be walking into the wind.'

'It is not as bitter as my remembrance.'

As we return to Cheapside, I watch my younger self arriving at Bedlam. I am nonplussed. I have not thought of the visit in what . . . four, five, maybe six years? Yet the scene is as fresh in my mind as if I had played it on the stage a dozen times. At the portal, Sir George explains that the sculptures on the pediment represent the two types of inmate: Melancholia, his face as drained of expression as his mind is of thought; Raving Madness, raging against the chains that bind him. Papa, who seeks to cultivate Sir George, praises the power of the figures, but Mama is apprehensive about their effect on me.

'Are you sure that the spectacle is suited to a boy of such tender sensibilities?'

'Your solicitude does you credit, madam,' Sir George says, 'but Master Betty is no callow stripling. Will the youth who inspired the Peruvian army to drive out the invaders – and caused Lady Beaumont to forget herself so utterly that she rose to her feet and shrieked her approbation like a Billingsgate – be afeared of a company of madmen?'

I gaze up at the statues and wish, not for the first time, that I had Rolla's spirit. Sir George, meanwhile, summons the porter who, after pocketing his pourboire, leads us into a dismal grey quadrangle, whose very stones are enough to make me shudder. Our guide, feeling no such disquiet, informs us that 'Our visit will be far more agreeable now that the rabble with their tuppeny contributions have been banished.'

The governor comes out to greet us, leaving me until last, less from propriety than awkwardness. He betrays the same mixture of awe and apprehension as I did on meeting Mr Kemble. 'Let me shake you by the hand, sir. Indeed, sir, yes. I saw your Tancred at Covent Garden last week. Remarkable . . . quite remarkable. I am not ashamed to admit that I wiped away a tear . . . yes, sir, a tear.' I mumble my thanks. He finally releases my hand and leads us up the stairs, repeatedly looking back as if to be sure that I have not vanished. We enter a vast, ill-lit gallery, where those whose alienation of mind is deemed to be inoffensive are permitted to congregate. We pass one who clings to the wall, as if it were we who posed the danger, and another who squats on his heels and rocks. I gaze at the ten or twelve unfortunates, their heads shorn and clothes shabby, who populate the gallery, either walking, standing or sitting on the benches which line its walls, and observe that they are all men.

'The women are in the other wing,' the governor says. 'You must not forget that our inmates are moral defectives. No herdsman would keep rams and ewes in the same pen. Begging your pardon, madam.'

Mama's thin smile suggests that she is loath to grant it.

At the governor's instigation, a basketman brings over three inmates, one by one, to discourse with us. The first, of whom the governor appears peculiarly proud, was once an actor at Drury Lane and, when pressed, he will recite extempore. To Sir George's disappointment and my relief, he declines to do so. 'I am not in voice today. Besides this house is unworthy of me. Tag-rags and skipjacks! I have played before the king.'

As if to bear out his claim, the basketman pushes forward a man who professes to be the king. Sir George, who has encountered him before, gives him a sweeping bow before presenting me.

'This is young Master Betty, sire. You will recall being introduced to him at Drury Lane.'

'Nonsense. I have not ventured to the playhouse in many a year.'

'Surely you are mistaken? Did you not tell me, William, that you met the king?'

'Yes, I thought so,' I reply hesitantly, unwilling either to offend Sir George or distress the inmate.

'That impostor! That charlatan!' the deluded man shouts. Mama stifles a scream as the basketman approaches him with his stick, but the threat alone is enough to daunt him. 'You have been gulled. Are you not aware that the man is a lunatic? They have had to immure him in my castle of Windsor.'

'So why are you immured here?' Sir George asks him, with a wink at me.

'Why, for my own protection,' he replies, as if it were Sir George who had lost his wits. 'There are Jacobins abroad. There is one upstairs. He shot at me, but I survived. Mr Pitt insisted that I seclude myself for the sake of the nation. Where would my people be without their king?'

Whatever his objections to the impostor wearing his crown, he, like the actor, grabs the brand new sixpenny piece that Sir George gives him to buy tidbits (fruit or cheese, but not sweetmeats, which might inflame his passions). The basketman leads up the third inmate, whose disdain for the like gratuity becomes clear when he harangues us with an account of how Buonaparte's spies have infiltrated the Mint and impregnated both banknotes and coins with an invisible poison to infect the entire populace. Sir George gives him a handkerchief.

We walk down the gallery, past locked doors on either side. Several of the wickets are shut, and I try to envisage the cells behind them from the murmurings, shrieks and, most sinister of all, silences. Others are open and, braving the stench, I peer in to study the occupants, some of whom are pinioned in strait waistcoats and others who are under mechanical restraint. One man rattles the grille, tears streaming, as he repeatedly shrieks that 'They have murdered Percy.' Horrified, I ask the governor if Percy is his son, his brother or his friend.

'Do you suppose us such monsters?' he asks. 'It was the rat who lived in his cell.'

I gaze in bewilderment at a man who confers his affection on vermin. Then, casting an envious glance at Mama, who elects to stay behind, I accompany the men to the second floor, where the most dangerous inmates are confined. It appears that, like Hamlet's, there is method in the uncrowned king's madness, for the governor takes us to visit the failed regicide, who did indeed take aim at King George and, moreover, did so in the theatre. Lying in the dark, fettered to the bed in an atmosphere as noxious as the Monkey Room at the Tower, he looks more pitiful than traitorous. He shields his eyes from the light as we enter.

'Spruce up, Hadfield,' the governor says, shaking the bed. 'You have visitors.'

'Leave me be! Must you ever torment me?'

'Do you complain, you villain?' Sir George says. 'Had I been the judge, you would have been put to the torture and hanged at Newgate, not left to idle your days on the public purse. I saw you! I was there, at Drury Lane on the night that you sought to kill our noble sovereign as he entered his box.' Sir George's voice cracks with emotion. 'I was witness to his valour when, once you had been apprehended, he summoned the queen and princesses to join him and they sat to watch the play, as if your outrage had been a planned prelude. You should have been executed on the spot.' The governor looks uneasy when Sir George takes a step towards the miscreant, as if to redress the oversight. 'But no, the judge heard testimonies that you were a devoted father, who had tried to kill your child two days before. So he declared you mad.'

'That is well-reasoned,' Hadfield says. 'To kill a child would be madness, but to kill a king is sanity.'

'You blackguard!'

'Sir George, please,' the governor says. 'Hadfield, you are honoured. I have brought the Young Roscius to meet you.'

Hadfield looks at me slowly and spits. 'You have brought a boy here to bait me?'

'It is not a boy; it is Master Betty.'

'Master . . . mistress: it is all the same to me.'

'I have not come to bait you, sir,' I say.

'You have or you have not: it is all the same to me. Tell me, boy, do you have a father?'

'I do, sir. He is standing by the door.'

'Ah yes, another baiter. And did he fight in the war?'

'No, sir, but he put down the Irish rebels.'

'Chicken stake! Tell him to try being one of the Duke of York's orderlies, wounded in Flanders. Broken cheek, broken head, broken arms and left for dead for three hours in a ditch. Taken prisoner and kept half-starved for four years by the French. And when I was freed? What then? No recompense, no assistance, not one farthing from the king for whom I had shed my blood. Tell me, is it madness to have sought retribution?'

'Come away, William,' Sir George says, as we leave Hadfield to the brooding silence. 'What greater proof of insanity can there be than that the insane do not think themselves afflicted?'

We return to Mama, who awaits us anxiously at the foot of the stairs.

'There, madam, I told you that he would come to no harm.'

'Do not trouble yourself, Sir George,' Papa says. 'She cossets him shockingly.'

'Quite understandable, I dare say. But I am sure that William would agree that he has been both entertained and edified. A caution to control his passions, except of course those that he exhibits on the stage for the benefit of us all.'

Sir George's voice lightens into Northcote's. 'You look despondent, Betty,' he says as we walk back down Ludgate Hill.

'It is just the drizzle,' I reply casually, as I ponder the appeal of losing my reason, not to be locked in my cell like Hadfield, but to wander the gallery like my fellow actor, free from duty, ambition and, most welcome of all, memory. It would be a kind of self-murder, but one for which I bore no guilt. I cannot pretend that oblivion holds no attraction. Indeed, there were times at Christ's when I wished that my paper knife had been a dagger. Harness once entered to find me caressing my throat with its ivory blade. Happily, his ignorance of my stage career, along with suspicions of my weak character, enabled me to persuade him that I was re-enacting one of my old roles. 'Hamlet?' he proposed, and I concurred, although, unlike Hamlet, I was deterred less by the fear of what lay ahead than the pain I would cause to those left behind.

Having accompanied me back to my lodgings, Northcote returns to fetch me for dinner two hours later. Once again, I solicit the name of our host or hostess and, once again, he equivocates, replying only that it is my greatest admirer and his own most munificent patron. I picture the Duke of Clarence, the Duchess of Devonshire, Lord Abercorn, Sir George Beaumont and a host of others, but I cannot recall whether they were his supporters as well as mine. Then, as the carriage turns into Brook Street, I feel as queasy as I did crossing the Irish Sea as a boy. I remember that long before Northcote painted me, I saw several of his portraits at Browsholme Hall. My suspicions are confirmed when we draw to a halt outside a tall white house, the elegantly planted white-and-purple window gardens of cyclamen, heather and ivy evincing its owner's much vaunted taste. I am as angry with myself for my discomfiture as with Northcote for colluding in the mystery. If tomorrow I am to stand on the stage in front of three thousand people, then tonight I must surely be able to dine with the Bow-bearer of the Forest of Bowland.

A footman admits us to the hall, which is lined by four of his fellows. I am reminded of the suits of armour that adorned the stairwell at Browsholme, relics of the Civil War, although, as the Bowbearer explained, his ancestors had escaped the conflict, having secured letters of protection from the opposing militias. There is a moral in there somewhere, if only I could apprehend it. Meanwhile, I take the measure of a man for whom displays of antiquities and servants are interchangeable. We are conducted up to the drawing room, where the Bowbearer, exquisitely dressed in a jade green coat, buff waistcoat and white silk breeches, with a large emerald in his neckcloth, waits to greet us. His chestnut curls lie less luxuriantly on his brow and his rosy cheeks owe more to the powder pot than when we last met, but in all other respects he is just as I remember.

'Master Betty, as I live and breathe.'

Northcote turns, as if expecting me to correct him, but I say nothing, preferring to confine him to my past.

'I would never have known you. You have brought back

so much more of yourself to delight your devotees. Pray be seated. Will you take a glass – no, not there!' he shouts, as I make to sit on a small cane armchair. 'Pray do not think me discourteous, but the chair was my mother's favourite. It is exceedingly fragile. I fear that it may not withstand the strain.' I feel the heat rising in my cheeks and trust that it is anger and not shame. 'Fetch that chair for Master Betty,' he commands the footman, who drags an ornately carved oak chair from the corner of the room. 'This is the chair on which Lady Jane Grey sat while awaiting execution. I trust that you are not superstitious.'

'You have refurbished the room since my last visit,' Northcote says, seeking to steer the discourse on to a gentler path.

'You speak of the tapestries?' He points to two large hangings of exotic birds in verdant settings. 'The finest Aubusson. My agents acquired them last year from a French duke – delicacy prevents my naming him – who was in pressing need of funds.'

'But we are at war. How did you transport them across the Channel?'

'Antwerp, my dear fellow. With the exercise of ingenuity, anything can be transported through Antwerp. Such as the excellent claret and brandy you will be offered at table. And the new Sèvres service off which we shall dine. We must not let the clash of arms inhibit the pleasures of fashion.'

I, whose last visit to the room long predates Northcote's, am aware of one particular change. Where there is now an ebony-and-gilt chest, the front panel enamelled with lilies and roses, there was once a cabinet or, as the Bowbearer put it with no trace of irony, an altar, decked with memorabilia of my performances. There were commemorative medals and fans, teapots, cups and paper dolls, Selim turbans and Norval caps, and a profusion of snuff boxes depicting my various characters. The Bowbearer, of course, had the complete set, filling each with differently scented snuff; I remember rose in Romeo and, I think, bergamot in Selim and jasmine in Norval. He turned a tribute into a threat when, with a gesture as practised as any player's, he took a box from his waistcoat pocket, flicked it open with his thumb and, with a whisper of a wave, lifted it to his nose. 'You see, William,' he said, 'I keep you next to my heart and then, with one pinch, I breathe you into my very soul.'

I shudder. 'Are you cold, sir?' the Bowbearer asks. 'Heaven forfend that you should be taken ill before your first performance!'

'It is nothing. Footsteps over my grave.'

'I trust that they are not those of a critic. Shall we eat?'

He leads us into the dining room, which is dominated by portraits of the Bowbearer and his mother, a lady who, as I recall, deemed that a wry smile at her son's eccentricities sufficed to rob them of offence.

'You used to hang a portrait of me,' I say, to my instant regret.

'No doubt it is in some lumber room or other,' he replies, his nonchalance negated by his knitted brow. 'It is only natural that Master Betty – forgive me, the erstwhile Master Betty – should cling to past glories. The rest of us have moved onwards.'

He indicates our seats: Northcote, to his surprise, is on his right, and I am on his left. The first course is a white soup, which I do little more than stir around my bowl. Northcote, while eating heartily, asks whether we are to be joined by other guests, since the table is set for twelve.

'Alas no! I asked; I begged; I went down on bended knee to some of those who had known Master Betty in his salad days – I do not say *heyday*, for that is surely still to come – but, to a man, they declined. What is more, they offered such feeble excuses. One said that he was testing a new neckerchief; another that he never went abroad on a day beginning with a T. So we are left to dine confidentially.' He addresses me. 'I trust that it will not be too grave a disappointment.'

'Not at all,' I say, wondering why, given my many grievances against the Bowbearer, he should be goading me.

At my host's insistence, I take slices of sturgeon, mutton, and pigeon pie, nibbling where I would usually devour.

'Do you recall the dinner I gave in honour of both your and Opie's portraits of the Young Roscius?' he asks Northcote, with a show of casualness.

'You made us into rivals.'

'You were rivals.'

'But never before with the same subject in the same exhibition.'

I too recall the dinner, when he made me stand on a plinth between the portraits and demanded of each guest in turn which of the three was the most beautiful. I cringed as, without exception, they picked the original rather than the copies, whereupon he insisted on making his own choice. I can still hear the venom in his voice when he opted for either of the canvases, indifferent as to which, because they were not ungrateful: they did not answer back or complain about being left alone with him. I take a large mouthful of mutton, content to know that I wounded him, if only a fraction as deeply as he did me.

'You tried to have them both removed from the Academy,'

Northcote says. 'Opie, more forthright than I, protested at the restriction, and the paintings were reinstated and hung, a few feet from each other, in the Great Room.'

'As they are now in the hall of my house in Shropshire,' I interject. 'At my mother's instigation, not mine.'

'And there you have it,' the Bowbearer says. 'I gave the portraits and all the rights in them to Mr Betty. It was he who ordered their removal. He had engaged Heath to engrave them and feared that prior exhibition would reduce the demand for prints. Your father had a rare talent for amassing money.'

'And for losing it,' I reply. 'As you should know, having introduced him to the faro tables at your club.'

'If not me, then it would have been someone else. And I doubt that he or they would have been so scrupulous about preserving your fortune. It was I who persuaded your father to put a portion of your earnings (what a tawdry word!) into trust, so that he could not run through it in the way that he had broken the entail on your mother's estate.'

'The estate was entailed?'

'I ever had your interests at heart. And how did you repay me? Were it not for me, you would be living in penury.'

'You said that he broke the entail. How?'

'Enquire of your mother. What is it to me? I have had my fill of the Betty family and its paltry affairs.'

Why should I ever know my father, if he is a villain? My heart is satisfied with a mother.

'I intend no slur on this excellent repast,' Northcote says, 'but it has the air more of a wake than a celebration. I assured Mr Betty that he would be welcomed by his most steadfast admirer.'

'Which of us would that be? You, who immortalised his

youth and beauty and refused to censure his acting, even when the whole town mocked you. So that your constancy was held to be higher than your judgement.'

I gaze in gratitude at Northcote.

'Or I, who followed him around the country to towns that had never before known a gentleman of fashion, my pocketbook open to his father at every turn. And what did I receive for my pains? Nothing, but like Hamlet, to "eat the air, promise-crammed." Nevertheless, I am of a forgiving disposition and shall be in my box at six tomorrow to cheer you on. I have paid no heed to the reports of your reception elsewhere.'

'What reports? I was much favoured. It is true that the houses were small.'

'You are among friends, sir. Accuracy is an imperative; they were *minuscule*. But no doubt there were contending attractions: perhaps a performing pig or a limbless fiddler? Tomorrow, you will have the town to yourself – that is, apart from Drury Lane and Astley's and the Adelphi and the Pantheon and the Lyceum. But what do they matter? The legend of Master Betty lives on. Although I trust that, leaving nothing to chance, you have stationed ringers judiciously through the house to lead the applause.'

'I never thought . . . Should I have? Is that the practice?'

'I fear that that is a grave misjudgement. Did you learn nothing from Mr Hough?'

'Mr Hough would never have resorted to such subterfuge. He believed in me.'

'I have no doubt that he did. The question is what it was that he saw in you.'

What a handsome boy!

The phrase resounds in my ears and I cover them with

my hands. Northcote looks perplexed and the Bowbearer amused, as I clumsily switch to swatting a fly.

'I know what he saw in you,' I say, reduced to tit for tat.

'A man as dedicated to your service as he was himself,' the Bowbearer replies. 'A man who put all that he possessed at your disposal: a man ready to risk his friendships . . . his reputation on your behalf.'

'Then why did he distrust you so much?'

'He could not stomach a rival.'

'What rival? He was my tutor; you were . . .'

'Yes, what was I? Tell me.'

'You were his friend,' Northcote interjects. 'We all were. We all are. Good friends.' He signals to the footman to fill his glass.

'You thought that you could use and discard me at will,' the Bowbearer says. 'But you reckoned without your father's weakness.'

'What do you mean?'

'Cards. He lost so much at the faro table. He gambled away half your wealth. Norval, Tancred, Romeo on a single draw. But there were those who took pity on him, who had no wish to see him ruined, who tore up his promissory notes on the promise of a greater intimacy with his son.'

'I am not sure that I wish to hear—' Northcote says.

'Lever, pour Mr Northcote another glass. You will hear it, sir. You will hear a tale of base ingratitude that would make even Scipio weep.'

I clutch the table to stop myself shaking. I see him once again in the dressing room, from which I had begged that he and his friends be permanently banished. Papa derided my diffidence, declaring that Mr Brummell, the Prince's boon companion, invited favoured guests to watch him at his morning toilet and that the greatest nobles in France had vied for the honour of attending King Lewis at stool. Since the crush to see me was always so great, this was an occasion for certain men of rank, my special friends, to salute me. I had no rebuttal, and I doubt that one would have made any difference. So I sat, squirming on the couch, while Papa pulled off my shirt and stockings, damp and clinging to my skin after the evening's exertions, and handed them to the enraptured spectators, who joked about touching the hem of my garments, except that they not only touched them but clasped them to their noses and lips. I lay helpless while Papa rubbed liniment on my back and, suddenly, the strokes felt softer. Had he delegated the task – the privilege – to one of the company? Might it have been the Bowbearer himself? I need to know.

'Did my father not fulfil that promise? In my mind's eye, I see you with a bevy of beaux, crowding into my room at the end of every performance.'

'Sometimes I came with friends, yes; but sometimes alone. Do you not see us alone?'

'And I should leave you alone to reminisce,' Northcote says.

'Ingratitude, Northcote!' the Bowbearer says. 'There is no graver sin. In the words of the holy carpenter, it is the one that cannot be forgiven.'

'Yes, I see us alone,' I say, as my memory gapes open like an ill-stitched wound. 'You put your hand on my chest.'

'To undo the buttons of your shirt. You were hot.'

'People always say that acting must be hard, but most of all it is hot.'

'I rest my hand on your heart. I feel it beating like a bird. I ask if you ever held a bird in your hand.'

'No!'

'Correct, you say "no".'

'No, I do not recollect.'

'My recollection is clear enough for both of us. I kneel down to remove your stockings. I make myself a servant for you. I, the Bowbearer of the Forest of Bowland, an office older than that of Earl Marshall, am become your valet. And what do you do? You grab your stage foil and point it at me. I tell you that it is blunted, and you answer that the edge is still sharp. And I have the scar to prove it.' He turns to Northcote. 'Do you wish to see it?'

'No! And I wish to hear no more. I must leave you.' He scrapes back his chair.

'Ingratitude!' the Bowbearer shouts. 'Must I charge you with it too, after all the employment I have brought you?'

Northcote sits bolt upright. I recall – no, I relive – the episode. Every part of me feels raw, as if he is ripping off my skin along with my clothes. 'It was not just my stockings,' I say.

'Mumble, mumble! Speak up! How will you ever hope to reach the boxes, let alone the gallery?'

'It was my breeches.'

'So you said. Believe me, sir, as the innocent victim you lacked conviction. You who, as Osmond, had just sought to ravish your ward Anna.'

'Angela,' Northcote interjects.

'Anna, Angela, what does it import? You were no virginal Miss de Camp fleeing from ruttish Mr Kemble. Yet the act you put on when Mr Hough walked in was as good as anything you ever did on the stage.'

'It was no act!'

'But then it was nothing to the one that Hough himself

put on. Imprecations! Threats! While you clung to him, snivelling. The hypocrite! What he could not brook was that I had dared to attempt what he was too pigeon-hearted to do himself.'

'It is no matter to boast of, sir,' Northcote says.

'He summoned your father. The arch-hypocrite! He knew what comprised your appeal, even if Hough did not. Even if Hough had managed to convince himself, as he had countless others, that you were indeed Garrick reborn, Mr Betty was under no such illusions. Would I really have torn up a note for ten thousand pounds in exchange for a few honeyed words?' His face and voice assume a tortured expression. 'He threatened to call me out should I ever approach you again, so I withdrew. And I took my friends with me. I am not one to blow my horn, but I like to think that my defection played a part in your swift and bloody demise.'

'I am not dead, sir.'

'I speak metaphorically. And you an actor! My one consolation is that no sooner had your father dismissed me than he dismissed Hough. He was no friend of mine (far from it!), nevertheless I felt for him. To be treated so shabbily! I never understood why. I knew your father to be a brute and a braggart, but I never took him for a fool. Would you do me the kindness of explaining what occurred?'

'Some matters are private.'

I have no intention of revealing what I know about the breach and even less of admitting what I do not. The sequence of events is as jumbled as a game of jack-straws. The Bowbearer's expulsion emboldened Mr Hough to restrict my visitors after the play and to oppose Papa's demands that I attend – let alone perform at – receptions when I was fatigued. They quarrelled repeatedly over my stock of roles, with Mr Hough preferring to keep me in the youthful ones that were ever the most admired, and Papa wishing to extend my range. He had spoken to Mr Kemble, who was eager for the town to appreciate my versatility as Shylock, Cato, Sir Giles Overreach, and even Othello, which had been one of Garrick's rare failures. Mr Hough protested, warning that Mr Kemble was intent on destroying me, whereupon Papa accused him of paying lip-service to my talent and, worse, wanting to keep me in boyish roles to indulge his own perversity (I raise my napkin to my lips, lest the Bowbearer see me blanch). Their clashes grew more and more heated, until Papa declared that, if Mr Hough were unwilling to prepare me for new roles, there was no purpose to his remaining my tutor. Horrified, I insisted that he still had much to teach me about the old roles, prompting Papa to banish me from the room with a ferocity that I had not witnessed in him since Ireland. Pride as ever proved to be Mr Hough's frailty and, rather than attempting to compromise, he packed his valise and departed that same afternoon.

Try as I might, I cannot recall his coming to say farewell. He must have done so, but I cannot recall it.

'You are silent, Mr Betty,' the Bowbearer says. 'In which case you leave Mr Northcote and myself no alternative but to think the worst.'

'Pray do not think on my behalf, sir,' Northcote says. 'I may be your guest but I am my own man.'

'A laudable reply. Lever, more wine for Mr Northcote! But I remain at a loss. Shortly after your father dismissed him, a notice appeared in several newspapers under the curious heading of *Hough versus Betty*, with an under-title of *An appeal to the British Public* or suchlike, in which your former tutor promised to lay bare the truth behind your triumphs. Yet no article ever followed. He withdrew all his threats in return for a small annuity of what was it – fifty pounds a year?'

'So I am told.'

'Did he really rate his contribution that low? Or was he afraid of your father's rejoinder?'

'Such as?'

'That his services to you were more than pedagogic.'

'It is late,' I say, pushing back my chair and standing. 'I must thank you for the meal. I fear that I have failed to do it justice.'

'Of course, he may have realised that the game was up. Folly had consumed the town like wildfire. But even the fiercest fire burns itself out in time. And what is left?' He pulls a candle towards him and snuffs it. 'You were the most beautiful boy that any of us had ever seen. A beauty of such transcendence that it blinded us to all else: not just our own deficiencies, but yours. Where is that beauty now?'

'On my canvas,' Northcote interjects.

'True. And in here,' the Bowbearer taps his brow. 'In my memory. Even now, fat and sweating as a pot boy, you cannot take that from me.'

'Mr Northcote, I bid you goodnight.'

'Do you wish me to accompany you? I owe you an apology. This evening was not as I had been led to expect.'

'You are most kind, but I prefer to go alone.'

'My carriage is at your disposal,' the Bowbearer says.

'Thank you, but you have done too much already. I need to clear my head.'

'Of course, tomorrow is the day of reckoning. My box will be brimming with your quondam friends.'

'I do not doubt it.'

I leave the house and make my way back to Covent Garden. The streets are deserted in the November mists and, with dampness seeping through my coat and shoes, I almost regret not having accepted the offer of the carriage. But I need the walk to put a distance between the Bowbearer and myself. I knew that I had good reason to hate him, but until just now I had forgotten exactly what it was. Why? Why is it that I should recall trifles like the Carlton House carpet and not something of such moment? It cannot be because of the foulness of the souvenir or else I would have forgotten the pigs eating the rebels in Ballynahinch and the inmates lying in their filth in Bedlam. Besides, he is the one who bears the scar from our last encounter, when I seized the stage foil and sliced the hand that he sought to insinuate into my drawers. I commend myself for confronting him both then and now. Nothing could have hurt him more than to show him how little he meant to me. So it is no surprise that he has grubbed for calumnies.

Yet what price victory if it costs me my faith in Mr Hough?

Footsore, I arrive at the lodgings where I am admitted by the yawning maid, who informs me that the rest of the household is abed. I tap on Mama's door and am heartened by the homely figure, in nightshift and curl papers, who greets me. Pressing her finger to her lips and looking carefully to left and right to ensure that there is no one in the vicinity to observe her dishabille, she follows me to my room at the back of the house. I apologise for rousing her and explain that I have been gravely disturbed by something I heard at dinner. I note her shudder at my naming of the host but choose to ignore it, since my concern is Mr Hough.

'Were you there when Papa dismissed him?'

'Your father never discussed his affairs with me.'

'The Bowbearer said that he threatened to put his case before the public, but he withdrew it on the offer of a fifty pound annuity.'

'It was so long ago.'

'Eight years. Why did he change his mind? Had he done – or rather did Papa suspect him of doing or even wishing to do – something that would have dishonoured him?'

'This is not what should be occupying your mind on the night before the performance.'

'I need to know, Mama. It is so hard to talk about it, especially to you, but I have no one else. He scarcely touched me. He seemed almost frightened to do so. When he told me to stand up straight, he would draw his cane down my spine. When he gave me gestures, he would demonstrate rather than manipulate. Even so, critics called me his puppet! But after he left us, he tried to bring out another boy, a Master Wilson. Did you know that?'

'I may have. It is late, William. I am too tired to think clearly.'

'He has a lisp, Mama, this Wilson. And thinning hair. Nonetheless, I suppose he would be accounted personable. Was that what Mr Hough saw in him? Was that what he saw in me?'

'He admired you so much, from the moment he saw you.'

What a handsome boy! 'Yes, I remember his very first words to me.' I do not repeat them.

'Many is the time I have wished that Papa had never chanced upon him at the racecourse. Do you think he would have permitted the two of you such daily proximity had he harboured the least suspicion of his character? Nor, in despite of the hullaballoo he unleashed, can I find fault with Mr Hough's behaviour towards you. The reason he abandoned his case was the fear of hurting you. That is the long and the short of it, for all of Mr Parker's venom.'

'Would you swear to that on my . . . on Marianne's life?'

'What is this?' She stares at me in dismay. 'Do you no longer trust me?'

'Not you, Mama, but your memory. I have discovered how defective that organ can be.'

'That is because you lack sleep.' She moves to the bed and runs her hand between the sheets. 'Good. I told the girl to use the warming pan. Make haste while there is still heat.'

'But if you had heard the Bowbearer . . . he was in deep earnest. And his charge corresponded so closely to Wilson's.'

'Malice speaks with many tongues but a single voice.'

'Is that from a play?'

'Not to my knowledge. Why?'

'Because it is so true. I knew that the answer lay within my grasp. Do you remember when I was a boy and you drew the poison from my boil with a poultice of bacon fat?'

'Ask me again in the morning.'

'Now you have drawn the poison from my mind. I have been prey to such torments ever since Wilson challenged me in Liverpool. But now they are disappeared.'

'I am glad, dearest.'

'Pah! See, all gone!'

'Very glad. Now it is time for us both to sleep.'

She walks to the door.

'I know it grieves you that I quit Christ's without taking my degree,' I say, loath for her to leave.

'You brought Papa great comfort in his dying days.'

'But I have not forgotten my bible study. As Elihu said to Job, a man whose sorrows far exceeded mine, it matters not if nine hundred and ninety-nine men accuse you, provided that there is one honest man to intercede for you. I see now that Mr Hough is that man.'

'Oh William!' Mama cups her hand over her mouth and rushes from the room.

He is that man. I would stake my life upon it.

7

I scour the accounts of my London debut eight years ago to find that I was greeted 'with every mark of approbation from a brilliant house;' I was received with 'the greatest plaudits that have ever been bestowed by any audience;' moreover, 'the ovation was tumultuous and those who came to censure remained to praise.' Should I ever prepare these pages for publication, no doubt my readers will be expecting a similar tribute from the present audience. After journeying with me from Bath in February (and, indeed, from Ballynahinch nine years ago), they – or might it now be *you*? – will be hoping that, just as at the conclusion of a well-judged novel the hero is rewarded for his tribulations with a large fortune or a noble wife or both, so all my remembrance and rumination will not have been in vain and I will have regained my command of the stage and my place in the affections of the public. In which case, I regret that I have to disappoint you. There was no ruckus: no orange peel and apple cores, no boos and hisses (at least none that reached my ears); there was only indifference. The house was indifferent; the applause was indifferent; and I fear that, in consequence, my performance was indifferent.

I repeated Selim the following Monday, added Osman on Wednesday, and am to play Essex tonight, which will no doubt be as indifferent as the rest. Although the pit and the gallery have been passably full, the boxes are half-empty with no trace of the bon ton. Friends have been consolatory. Northcote, eager to disassociate himself from the Bowbearer's masquerade, has come to every performance: the first, with his fellow painter, Mr Fuseli, who declared me to be a 'sans pareil'. Mr Godwin attended my return as Osman and assured me that I had it in me to surpass Mr Kemble, which was generous indeed, given that he had written an Italianate tragedy expressly for me, which Mr Hough had deemed inferior and refused to let me play. Familial praise is to be expected, but Mama and Marianne have been most appreciative. Mama brought Mrs Stirling to *Zara*, the landlady informing me afterwards that, although she lived a stone's throw from the theatres, she had always resisted letting rooms to actors, but my performance had persuaded her to reconsider. Since I was playing a Mohammedan sultan who stabs first his Christian lover and then himself to death, that was no mean feat.

After breakfasting alone in the coffee house, I make my way to the theatre where, with time pressing, Mr Farron has arranged the group rehearsal of *Essex* to follow straight after the two partial ones. It will come as no surprise that they are indifferent too. As I withdraw, Mr Farron informs me that Mr Kemble has arrived back from Ireland and would be obliged if I would call on him. The news invigorates me and I hasten to the manager's office, where he sits at a desk on which not a single paper is out of place. His brow is an inch or two higher than when last we met; his hair is flecked with grey; his face bears the spider veins of crapulence as well as the crow's feet of age; but his presence is imposing and his handshake firm.

He greets me with a *Mister*, which makes up for a score

of misplaced *Masters*, and trusts that I have found every-thing in the theatre to my satisfaction.

'Everyone has been most kind,' I reply, equivocally. He says nothing. 'I fear that you must be disappointed with the receipts.'

'They are much as I anticipated. You still have a follow-ing, of sorts. And I felt it my duty to engage you now that you stand among us as an equal, no longer bringing ridi-cule on the rest of the profession.'

'You have my word that it was never my intention to ridicule anyone.'

'No, I doubt that it was. You cannot be held responsible for all the mischief contrived in your name. You played the hero on the stage and the town played the fool off it. My own part in the affair was a tawdry one, and I am not proud of it. Tempers were frayed and harsh measures undertaken. I trust that you will pardon me.'

'Of course,' I say, baffled. 'But there is nothing to pardon.'

'Come, come, sir, let us abandon the pretence.'

'But I assure you, you were kindness itself.'

'You are no longer a child, sir. Either your time at the university has done nothing to sharpen your wits or else you are deliberately affronting me.'

'Never!' I exclaim in horror. 'I have always held you in the highest esteem.'

'It was my sister whom you saw play in Belfast, not me.'

'But I saw you here, before the malady of your lungs kept you from the stage for the entirety of my two seasons.'

'Do you think that I would expose myself to derision: to be told to take instruction from an untutored boy . . . no, an all-too-carefully tutored boy? Better to bide one's time until the spell was broken.'

'It is only now, when I too am compared with a boy – the boy I once was – that I apprehend how vexing it must have been for you. Yet in despite of a severe cough (so severe that it was plainly audible from the stage), you attended several of my performances. As did Mrs Siddons. Her remark that I was a matchless genius outweighed all the other tributes I ever received.'

I blush, as Mr Kemble fixes me with a dumbfounded gaze. 'I fear that you are sincere and I have wronged you. Did your bear-leader, Mr Hough, never explain that a line could be uttered in many ways, at times to mean the very opposite of its semblance? In the era of your ascendancy – ' he spits out the word – 'my sister underwent an electric cure on her back. She described the impact of the sparks as like burning lead swirling beneath her skin. But even that did not cause her as much pain as sitting through one of your performances.'

'I see.' Although determined not to let him witness my despair, I find it harder to speak than if I were facing a volley of missiles from the gallery. 'I trust that her back is much improved.'

'Indeed it is.'

'What of you?' I ask, clenching my fingers. 'Did you also revile my acting?'

'I grant that attitudes were struck prettily, lines were spoken mellifluously, and points were made with vigour. But of conception of character, truth to nature and the revelation of man to man, which is the object of our art, there were none.'

'So was there nothing you admired?'

He pauses, either for reflection or effect. 'I admired your deaths.'

I quit the office and long to quit the theatre, but I have unleashed a flood of reminiscence and am borne along on its current. I pass through the stage door and find myself in the saloon, among the audience waiting for the boxes to be unlocked. Modest distinctions of hair and dress – the women with looser curls, piled higher on their heads, their gowns simpler and in lighter shades; the men with shorter whiskers and lower cravats, sporting larger lapels and more brightly hued waistcoats – apprise me that I am once again in my past.

My face and gait bespeak my excitement, as I make my way down the corridor. I am escorted by Papa, which surprises me, since it is usually Mr Hough who brings me here on nights when I am not performing. As I take my seat, my confusion increases for, from all sides, I hear whispers of 'The Young Roscia'. I wonder if it is an affectionate abbreviation of *Roscius*; but I am now well established in town and, to my relief, the days when my mere presence in the house would cause a furore have passed. Besides, all eyes are turned to the stage and I cannot be in two places at once . . . or so I thought before commencing this memoir.

A gentleman in the adjacent box addresses me across the partition. 'Well done, young sir, I commend your pluck. This must be deuced galling for you. They tell me she is only seven years old.'

'Not at all.' Papa answers for me, with a hint of menace in his voice. 'There will only ever be one Young Roscius. But it is a testament to my son's genius that Mr Kemble has sought to bring out other juvenile players, in the face of those who carp that he is turning the stage into a nursery. What was it you said this very morning, William?'

Quick on my cue, I cite the words Mama used to reassure me, which Papa has insisted I appropriate as my own. 'I am glad that other children can enjoy the same opportunities as me. I am not a boy who steals a plate of sweetmeats and gorges on them, without leaving any for his fellows.'

'Nicely put,' the man replies. 'It is as well not to be bitter.'

My younger self appears satisfied with the exchange, but I am more bewildered than ever. As I gaze at the playbill on Papa's lap, I find that the play is Garrick's *The Country Girl*. Scanning the cast list, I recognise several names: Mr Murray as Moody; Mr Charles Kemble as Harcourt; and Mr Brunton as Belville. Turning to the women, I see that Alithea is to be played by Miss Brunton and Peggy by Miss Mudie.

My heart hammers; my head swims; and I feel as if I have been punched in the teeth by Daniel Mendoza. So this is why I failed to recall where the performance took place. Over the past few months, I have had extensive evidence that my memory plays tricks, but never before have I had occasion to charge it with devilry. Why else has it obscured the diminutive figure of Miss Mudie? Why else has it obscured the moment when I looked into the glass and saw the face of a seven-year-old girl? Why else has it obscured the irony that my greatest theatrical battle occurred when I was off the stage?

I can no longer stand outside myself and am drawn fully into the scene, as Papa relates Miss Mudie's history. She started acting at her parents' theatre in Windsor and, during the past year, has been acclaimed for her comic characterisations in Liverpool, Dublin and Birmingham, to name but three. Papa, who worries unduly on my behalf, fears that the quality will transfer its allegiance to this new favourite, who is more precocious than I and of the weaker sex. He berates Mr Hough for neglecting to insert a clause in my contracts proscribing the engagement of younger actors. Then, mercurial as ever, he relents, reporting that, if the town takes to her, Mr Kemble plans to pair us as Romeo and Juliet. The prospect elates me since, in addition to the corporeal disparity, Mrs Litchfield is older than Mama. However much I strive to obey Mr Hough's injunction to envisage the beauteous, golden-haired Juliet, the image that obtrudes is that of Mrs Litchfield sans her wig.

The Country Girl opens with Peggy, ward of the jealous Moody, discovered in the parlour of her guardian's house, in conference with his sister, Alithea. Miss Mudie delivers her speeches passably, even if they smack of the multiplication tables and her consonants suffer from the absence of her top front teeth. I am perplexed that Mr Kemble did not choose a smaller companion for her than Miss Brunton or, at the very least, dissuade that lady from wearing an ostrich feather headdress, which elevates her by a good two feet. The imbalance between Miss Mudie and the rest of the cast is accentuated when Murray, as Moody, stoops to pat her head before bending double to kiss her. This elicits gales of laughter, which Murray misinterprets as his cue to pat her again. The house, although thin, is rowdy, and when at the end of the act, Moody informs Peggy that she will return to the country next week, a wag in the pit, heedless of how a casual jibe can fester in a player's mind, calls out: 'Why next week? Why not be rid of her at once?' This presages an even more brutal response in the third act when Moody, acceding to Peggy's demand to accompany her to the park, dresses her as a boy to shield her from the attentions of the gallants. Belville and Harcourt see through her disguise and, both to satisfy his own desires and humiliate Moody, Belleville busses her.

Having myself been subjected to the intimacies that men are licensed to bestow on their own sex, I condole with Miss Mudie, who suffers them by proxy, along with catcalls from an audience who blame her for the indelicacy. These increase a hundredfold when Belville and Moody pull her between them, her short stature and vacant countenance giving her the likeness of a rag doll. To the audience's delight and Miss Mudie's visible discomfort, Charles Kemble drops down on all fours to take hold of her, prompting further jeers. I fear that I alone feel pity for her plight, as she strives to make herself heard above the clamour. To my astonishment, she walks down to the floats and, with a self-possession that I could never hope to emulate, addresses the house in her own person: 'Ladies and gentlemen, I have done nothing to offend the company that is sent here to scoff at me and, I pray you, hear me out.'

Her fortitude stuns the audience and even draws several huzzahs, the loudest of which are mine, until Papa quiets me. But such tokens of appreciation are drowned out by another torrent of taunts. This is followed by a concerted cry of 'Manager', which Mr Kemble comes out on to the platform to answer.

'Ladies and gentlemen, I trust that I shall never be found wanting in my duty to the public. I assure you that the proprietors of the theatre had no wish to pass any species of spectacle which would incur their patrons' disapprobation. May I remind you of the indulgence that you have lately shown to other players of the juvenile genus and entreat you to permit the young lady to complete what will be positively her final appearance at the Theatre Royal.'

His supplication is in vain, and after an increasingly voluble expression of dissent, during which Miss Mudie remains admirably composed, the curtain is dropped. Mr Murray steps forward and announces that, Miss Mudie being indisposed, Miss Searle will assume her role for the remainder of the play. Her entrance is greeted by such resounding applause, with even her bungled lines being cheered, that one would have thought Mrs Jordan herself had returned in her best-loved character. Although sympathy for Miss Mudie makes me resent her replacement, I obey Papa's instructions to laugh and clap loudly, lest anyone should be watching. The moment that the curtain falls, he leads me out, without staying for the farce. He strides back to the lodgings so fast that I struggle to keep pace.

'Poor girl!' I say.

'Poor what?' He turns to me with a glint of fury in his eyes.

'Miss Mudie. They made a Shrove Tuesday sport of her.'

'God's blood! Miss Mudie is nothing . . . nobody . . . food for powder. The real target is you.'

'But I was not playing.'

'Did I not teach you that the best way to catch your opponent off guard was with a feint?' I am none the wiser. 'Hough was right about one thing; Kemble hates you. Fearing to hit at you directly, he has done so underhand. Did you not remark that "indulgence to other players of the juvenile genus"? To whom do you think it referred if not to you? That sorry spectacle will sanction all the nay-sayers. Henceforth, you will be easy prey.'

Although green room tattle had shown me that even capital actors were jealous of one another's fame, I refused to believe that Mr Kemble would mount a campaign against me, as though he were Richmond ridding the land of a loathed usurper. Nor could I believe that he would engage Miss Mudie to discredit me. Surely he had too much regard for the theatre that he and his sister had made their own? Or did he agree with the physicians, who deemed it prudent to cut off a limb in order to save a life?

On the surface, Miss Mudie's drubbing changed nothing. Mr Kemble encouraged Papa to bring me out in new roles: Warwick and Dorilas, neither of which showed off my strengths; and Oroonoko, which, perhaps more damagingly, failed to show off my face. In a compliment that I must now construe as a stratagem, he insisted that there was nothing more he could teach me, leaving Papa with a task for which he had neither the capacity nor the patience. Fearing disaster, I plucked up the courage to suggest that he recall Mr Hough.

'You were not there, William,' he replied, with unexpected mildness. 'You cannot understand. He accused me of such foul things.'

'What things?'

'I may not always have done what was right,' he said, disregarding the question, 'but I have always done what I thought was best. You do not know what it is to have a family.'

'I have a family: Mama and you and Marianne and Aunt—'

'A family for which you are responsible, not one which is responsible to you! I had needs of my own. Do you suppose that you are the only one with hopes and dreams and desires and ambitions? Please do not hate me, William. You are my son and I would never hurt you. Whatever anyone says, I never meant to hurt you.'

'Of course not, Papa,' I replied. How often had I longed for him to speak to me from the heart. Now that he had, I felt embarrassed. I sniffed to stem the tears that I knew he would scorn and asked him to test my lines.

Although the memory may be locked at the bottom of a strong box to which I have yet to find the key, I do not recall enduring an out-and-out attack such as Miss Mudie's but, rather, a gradual ebbing of support. At first, I was relieved at the absence of visitors to my dressing room and of invitations to carriage rides and receptions. I hoped to ply my trade like any other actor, but my age and repute made that impossible. Meanwhile, Mr Kemble enjoyed a near-miraculous recovery. After hacking so loudly through the final acts of *Oroonoko* that I muddled several speeches, he announced his return as Othello opposite Mr Cooke. I sat in the stage box and was as enthralled as the rest of the house by his performance. Even Mr Cooke, acknowledging the gravity of the occasion, remained strictly sober. At the end when the two adversaries, both on the stage and off, clasped hands, I shouted myself as hoarse as a postillion in a fog.

'Take care, William,' Mama said. 'You play Tancred tomorrow. You must preserve your voice.'

'You are as blind as he is,' Papa said. 'His voice matters little now.'

Looking back, it is as if I have spent my whole life in a stage box: so close to the players that I can almost touch them, yet with much of the scene hidden from view. Now I am standing at the rear of the gallery and, while the faces are indistinct, the broader picture is clear.

I sit in silence in my dressing room and listen to the preparations for the evening's performance. I am to play Essex and trust that the audience will cheer as my traitorous head rolls off the block. My detractors were right. I was not an actor but a sideshow. I should have set up a stall at Bartholomew Fair or turned cartwheels at Moorfields. That would have been no disgrace. Tumblers earn their daily bread just as I did, the difference being that they dived for farthings, while I was showered with sovereigns.

Is it such a misfortune to have known my greatest success as a boy? What law is it that states that we should steadily augment our achievements and that a sharp decline is, of necessity, a sad one? My critics expected me to be a man when I was still a boy, and objected to my playing roles that were beyond my grasp; my idolaters wish me to remain a boy when I am become a man, and complain that I have lost my youthful charms. In truth, I no longer care whether either or both are right. Having retrieved my memories, my one desire is to escape them.

The door is closed and there is no draught, yet my candle has blown out. I shall take it as a sign. Besides, it feels right to make my ultimate journey in the dark. But I am not alone. I feel so many others standing alongside me. The old stagers used to say that theatres were full of ghosts. I thought it was because I was a child and they were trying to scare me. After all, no one actually died; it was just a pretence. But now I know; it was not the characters that they meant but the players who, ousted by intrigue or dismissed by fashion, returned to haunt the scene. I put down my pen and pick up a knife – not a penknife nor a stage foil but a dagger. I tease the blade across my throat and test my resolution.

On what will be positively my final appearance at the Theatre Royal, I propose to give Mr Kemble one more death to admire.

POSTSCRIPT

Chester Terrace,
London

Thursday, 18 May 1837

My dear Madam,
I am much obliged to you for your gracious letter and
the enclosed pages, which I herewith return. I pray that
you will pardon my tardy response but, in recent weeks,
preparations for Mr Browning's *Strafford* have occupied my
every waking hour. I regret to relate that, notwithstanding
the best endeavours of the entire company, both before and
behind the scenes, the town has condemned the play to the
same fate as that of the eponymous earl.

I have read your son's chronicle with every care. Our
debased profession engenders much easy intimacy but little
genuine friendship, and I think fondly of the time that I
spent with him, both as a boy, when he was the cynosure
of all eyes, and later, when we acted together in Birmingham: I, at the dawn of my career, and he, although we
were not to know it, in the twilight of his. Having enjoyed
the society of a host of fine fellows at Rugby School, I was
saddened by his designation of me as his 'one boyhood

friend', although doubtless that attests to the singularity of his boyhood. Given his repeated interrogation of his memory, I am wary of lending too much credence to my own but, to the best of my recollection, he offers a faithful account of our youthful pranks and an accurate transcription of our adult discourse.

Like others of his friends – I use the word advisedly – I have had occasion to ponder his precocious triumphs and their effect on his later life. I was much distressed to read of his attempt at self-murder, which was widely reported at the time, not least by his fellow actors, who spread gossip around the country like the fleas in their clothing. I have to admit to ignorance of the second attempt, which in your account resembles a cross between a tragedy and a farce. After twenty-five years among the sock and buskin, I did not believe that my opinion of the profession could sink any lower, but I feel a deep repugnance on learning that only eleven of his former associates turned up to his gala dinner, bruising his confidence so severely that he threw himself from a first floor window. I give thanks that he ignored my advice to curb his appetite, since, from what you impart, his bulk was all that prevented his falling through the frame. I shudder to think of his humiliation as he dangled there to the relish of the crowd, until the constables succeeded in releasing him. You have my word that, had my calendar permitted, I would have been honoured to accept his invitation.

I knew that he had retired to the county of his birth and was relieved that the foresight of his trustees, together with your uncle's bequest, had afforded him the means to do so. My informants made no mention of his marriage, but I am delighted to hear of the erstwhile Miss Crow and the birth of their son, Henry (although it is hard to imagine the forever engilded youth as the father of a boy of seventeen!). I trust that your grandson offers you some consolation for the untimely death of your daughter, to whom, as I recall, her brother was devoted.

This brings me to the nub of your letter, and Mr Betty's plans to put Henry on the stage. Indeed, you remark that he has already appeared for one night in Gravesend in his father's old role of Selim. When, even with a granddam's fondness, you record his success as modest, I can only assume that the gentleman would be better suited to another occupation. I can barely contain my incredulity that, after all that happened to him, man and boy, Mr Betty should choose to bring out his son, who is but a few years older than he was himself on his debut. However, I have long since given up seeking to comprehend the motives of my fellow man, confining such speculation to my characters.

Although my heart was set on a career in the law, I confess that, as a boy, I felt a stab of envy for Master Betty and both the opportunities and the adulation he received. Having been obliged by indigence to tread the boards at a tender age, I am thankful that it was a decade before I gained renown. I have oft-times taken to task young actors in my company who, babes in arms during his prime, pour scorn on the ignorant audiences, avaricious managers and craven critics, who not only allowed a boy of twelve to play roles which were beyond his years and understanding, but lauded him immoderately for it. I explain that the roles may have been beyond his years and understanding, but they were not beyond his powers. I am convinced that, had circumstance and his own temperament permitted, Mr Betty had the capacity if not to be a second Garrick, then to become a capital actor.

Who knows what posterity will say of him: if, that is, posterity should concern itself with such fleeting matters as the stage? Will Mr Kemble's view – which, I admit, never wavered – prevail, or will mine? It is true that I was a mere boy, who had little scope for comparison, but time has done nothing to blunt the impact of his Norval, his Hamlet and his Selim. They will be forever etched on my memory until, to paraphrase Lear, my notion weakens and my discernings are lethargised.

You write that you chanced upon these pages in an attic chest and that Mr Betty knows neither that you have unearthed them nor sent them to me. Rest assured that I shall respect your confidence. The question you pose is whether, by showing them to your son and grandson, you might dissuade them from pursuing their imprudent theatric venture. My answer must be 'no'. I have been deeply disturbed to discover what was hitherto hidden in Master Betty's story, so I can only surmise how harrowing it would be for them: the father, who may once again have effaced its full horror, and the son, who would be confronted by his father's wrongs. Forgive my bluntness, but I doubt that a lady of delicate sensibility can be wholly cognizant of the wickedness that Mr Betty describes. Whatever humiliations he may heap on Henry and himself by this doomed attempt to relive (or redeem) his youth, reading this chronicle would surely exacerbate them. Indeed, now that it is back in your possession, I would urge you to take the first opportunity to consign it to the flames.

Believe me,
Yours most faithfully,
William Charles Macready

ACKNOWLEDGEMENTS

In writing *The Young Pretender*, I have adhered closely to what is known of Betty's life, while freely filling in the extensive gaps. During his brief heyday, Master Betty was the subject of numerous hagiographies, even the most sober of which is riddled with errors. A more authoritative memoir appeared in his middle years, when he had long since retired from the stage and his son Henry was pursuing his own acting career. Giles Playfair's *The Prodigy* (1967) remains the only posthumous biography. Jeffrey Kahan's *Bettymania and the Birth of Celebrity Culture* (2010) and Sandra Norton's unpublished doctoral thesis *William Henry West Betty, Romantic Child Actor* offer rich insights into the commercial exploitation of Betty's fame and his role in the nascent romantic movement, respectively. I am indebted to all these sources, as well as to many general studies of the period.

For help and advice on matters great and small, I am grateful to Katharina Bielenberg, Rupert Christiansen, Selina Hastings, Bruce Hunter, Piers Russell-Cobb, Milly Reid, Angeline Rothermundt and Corinna Zifko. I owe especial thanks to Luke Brown and Hilary Sage for their assistance with the text.